A DAUNTING ODYSSEY

FICTION

Kraftgriots

Also in the series (FICTION)

A DAUNTING ODYSSEY

FICTION

Chinwe Okoli

kraftgriots

Published by

Kraft Books Limited
6A Polytechnic Road, Sango, Ibadan
Box 22084, University of Ibadan Post Office
Ibadan, Oyo State, Nigeria
✆ +234(0)803 348 2474, +234(0)805 129 1191
E-mail: kraftbooks@yahoo.com;
kraftbookslimited@gmail.com
Website: www.kraftbookslimited.com

First published 2017

ISBN   978–978–918–450–7

= KRAFTGRIOTS =
(A literary imprint of Kraft Books Limited)

First printing, September 2017

Dedication

To my mum and grandmum

Appreciation

My deepest gratitude goes to God Almighty for his mercies and abundant grace.

My profound appreciation to Mr Ukoha Kalu who scrupulously read and edited the first draft of this work. God bless you always.

My warmest thanks to my family, my beloved mum and my dear grandma who are always there to inspire me. My entire family members—Bro Uzo, Bro Christopher, Austine (Half a million), Onyii, Ify, Ebere, Anuli Jnr, Uche, Ekene, Daniel, Ngozi, Gozie, Chukwudalu, Somtoo, God bless you all.

My special thanks to my father figure, Uncle UC. I am so blessed to have you as my guide and motivator. You know how to get me back on track always. God bless you and your lovely family.

To all the very special and amazing persons that have inspired me in many ways positive, Rev. Frs Linus Iloegesi, Vincent Nnabude, Chris Mmaduka, Prof. Chuma Ozumba, Dr Nkechi Onyeneho, Mr Geoffrey Ndubuizu, may God bless and reward you all.

Finally, my special appreciation to Mr Steve Shaba, my publisher; Oluchi, the editor, and all the staff of Kraft Books Limited. You are great at what you do and it is my pleasure working with you.

Prologue

Ijem is a third generation daughter of a widow who is struggling to make ends meet, and who is also bogged down by ill-health. She is a young and intelligent girl imbued with a focused determination to change a certain future which appears already doomed for her.

Sensing that the change could only come through self-help, and achieving a certain academic milestone, which is very uncommon to her forebears, she stubbornly persists in her quest, and refuses to settle for less in spite of what fate continuously doles out to her.

Sired in an unusual circumstance; in an ugly incident which the society frowns at, and stigmatizes its female victims, she craves for an elusive father, who is yet unknown to her while separated from her mother, Nneka. Now living with her grandmother, Nnedimma, she grapples with her grandmother's sickness – a debilitating ill-health, including poverty of the worst kind. Starting from age eleven she battles issues that are beyond her age.

Contending with life's vicissitudes in an African rural community setting; where she is pitched to be married off at the age of fourteen to an illiterate and older suitor, she resists and fights the idea of getting married at that age with an uncommon determination.

To ward-off what she sees as ill and misconstrued intentions, she engages her grandmother, uncles and aunties to a battle of her life ...

❦| *One* |❦

Wandering into the brushes around the precinct of the village for Ijem was not something she did by choice. It was more of an instinctive thing that she had gotten herself into for survival. For Ijeabalum, as her grandmother, Nnedimma, had named her at birth, as she wandered listlessly and lost in her own thoughts, loitering in the brushes at that moment appeared as the most logical thing for her to do. For sure, the brushes provided her the quietude and yet the opportunity to scavenge for their livelihood. Still besides herself, she had just remembered, and sadly too, that it was going to be another long vacation and which she was not enthusiastic about. She had also remembered that she had just turned eleven. It was early July and the next school year which starts in September would usher her into Junior Secondary School (JSS) 2. Her lack of enthusiasm and the sadness she was feeling at that moment was borne out of the fact that many of her fellow students would be going on holidays.

Some of them, as she was well aware, would be visiting cities like Lagos, Kano, Enugu, Abuja and Port Harcourt. But for her, it was going to be another, as they say, 'no leave and no transfer' situation. She was going to spend her holidays in the village as usual. She would have loved to visit somewhere, a city, but then as she had thought quickly, *who would she leave her frail and ailing grandmother to take care of? And even if such an opportunity had existed, where really would she have gone?* She sighed as she flailed her arms to shove aside some foliage which were interfering with her line of vision, and get rid of some of the jutted-out stems of wildly scattered shrubs which she had just walked into, absent-mindedly.

"*Chim ee*! Somebody help me, please!" Ijem's voice was heard screaming repeatedly in the bush. A while later, as quickly as she could get past the interfering thickets, she ran out of the bush in a frenzy, scratching her entire body in a disorderly manner. "*Chim ee!* My body, my back, my stomach, my ear... Somebody, please help me ..." She kept on screaming repeatedly, running both hands rapidly all over her itchy body. The few villagers who had heard the scream and gathered could not help. Not really knowing what the matter was with her, they kept their distance, looking on bemused and at the same time enthralled by the drama. Wasting a few seconds in their midst she took off again, running home under the scorching sun which even exacerbated her condition. She dashed into their compound calling out repeatedly in a loud voice, "Nne!"

Nnedimma sprang up on her feet regardless of her relatively old age; she was already far gone in her early sixties as she ran out to meet her screaming grandchild. Asking what the matter was with her, she inspected her body and discovered that the little girl had contracted *agbala,* the itchy plant in the bush. She dragged her quickly into the house and stripped her naked; and as an antidote, applied palm oil all over her body. Minutes later, the prickly feeling subsided. And then she made her to have a prolonged bath, ensuring that she lathered herself properly with the native black soap, *ncha nkota.*

Later that day, Nnedimma went out to the brushes to fetch fodder for the goats, and intentionally looked out for the itchy *agbala* plant with the intention of showing it to Ijem; so she would be able to identify and avoid it in the future whenever she strayed into the meadows.

After having sleepless nights over this particular issue that had bothered her so much, Nnedimma thought... *How do I explain this for her to understand? How do I make her see reasons with me? She is always singing about, 'school this, school that' and it simply shows how deeply she wants to continue going to school and her reverence for education. But what can a poor widow like me do? This little girl has passed through a lot in her young age. She has had a lot of bad experiences running through her tender heart. She has a very big and audacious dream bothering her little mind. I understand the craving of her little mind. But what can I do? What can I say? How do I approach it? From the look of things, anybody who dares contradict this dream of hers may be considered an enemy. What exactly do I do? How do I make her understand the situation of things?* Hmm! She heaved a sigh even as she continued agonising over the matter.

Nnedimma spent most of the night awake. She sat on the edge of her locally fabricated wooden bed, a contraption she had made with planks and woods placed on blocks she had retrieved from her neighbourhood. She sat awhile on the bed, still worried. She stood up suddenly prompted by a scratchy noise she had just heard. She looked up in search of the source of the noise. She seized the flickering *mpanaka,* a local lamp, which sat on the window's ledge burning and spewing swirls of smoke, to help her have a better view of whatever it was. She sighed. It was a rat chasing after another. The rodents had both ran out of her sight by the time she seized the stick that was always lodged within reach by her bedside. She practically dumped the lamp as she was already inhaling too much of the thick black smoke spewing from it. She stood hands akimbo as she surveyed the roof and the cracked red walled interiors.

It was a mud house which she had built in her youth. There was no ceiling and there were many cracks on the red wall making way for rodents to come in freely. Rats, snakes, lizards and wall geckos were common sight in the wall cracks. After a few minutes of wallowing in-between thoughts and imaginations, Nnedimma sat down and glanced at the peacefully

11

snoring Ijem. She wondered, *should I wake her up? No, maybe in the morning*. She laid down again but kept wide awake. In a moment, she sat up again and tapped the poor little girl, calling, "Ijem, Ijem, Ijem." The girl stirred in response but continued sleeping. She tapped and shook her a little bit violently. "Ijem, wake up, there is something I want to tell you." Ijem managed to sit up and wiped sleep off her eyes with the back of her hands.

"Nne, good morning," she said, yawning.

"Good morning, my daughter," replied Nnedimma.

"Nne, is it dawn already?"

"No, my dear, it's not yet dawn, I just want to tell you something," Nnedimma said.

"What is it, Nne? This thing that could not wait till morning, I am still feeling very sleepy."

Nnedimma stared at the obviously sleepy little girl and thought, *I am not sure I will sound coherent to her now given that she is still immersed in deep sleep. I think it should wait till morning.* "Don't you worry, Ijem, go back to sleep. We will talk about it in the morning," Nnedimma cooed. She barely finished the last word before the little girl laid back on the mat.

"Okay, Nne. *Kachifo,*" Ijem muttered, sleepily.

Early in the morning, Ijem got up as usual and swept the compound with the *akpata,* a long local broom. The compound was fenced. The fence was a dwarf mud wall, covered at the top with *igbegiri,* stumps of palm frond. The *igbegiri* is routinely replaced each time new ones are gathered during the dry season. The top-edge of the mud wall is beaten bumpy with a machete to enable the *igbegiri* to stay firm and withstand stormy winds. The *igbegiri* is intended to protect the wall from being soaked up during the rainy season because if soggy, the red mud wall would be prone to collapse in no time.

When she was done with the sweeping, she packed the

garbage with a basket and dumped the waste in the farm opposite their compound. Nnedimma sat on a local stool, commonly called *okpoga,* in front of the room on a mud-made pavement. She chewed on the remaining lobe of a kola nut she had shared with her neighbour who had called in that early morning to check on them. She brought out her snuff box and wiggled out a little into her left palm scooping enough with her right index finger and used the coffee-brown stuff to swipe across her teeth as if she was brushing her teeth with it. She repeated the sequence until the portion in her palm was exhausted. That was her own way of taking snuff. She then gargled, using her tongue to turn the mixture in her mouth until she was satisfied. *Poom*! She spat out the deep brownish mixture and sauntered back into her room.

"Ijem! Ijem! Ijem!" Nnedimma bawled.

"Ma!" came Ijem's long drawn response from the backyard where she was doing other household chores.

"Please, come, we need to talk."

Ijem swept aside the 'it was white' curtain that hung droopily at the entrance to their room. The formerly white coloured curtain had turned deep brown. It was draped there by Nnedimma when she was newly married; the reason was to shield away their privacy from passers-by. The mud house was built right on a busy pathway.

"Sit down, my daughter." She waved her to sit on an *okpoga*. Ijem sat facing her grandmother, wondering why she was thus summoned. Nnedimma placed her right hand on Ijem's shoulder and proceeded to advise her granddaughter. "See, Ijem, my daughter, please try to see reasons with me on this issue that I want to discuss with you. I want you to understand that I want the best for you. I want you to be happy, my dear. But you know that I am not doing any serious business at the moment to earn enough money. The reason is that my health is failing. I am no longer strong to struggle to pay your school fees. Please, my child, I am suggesting that you quit school. By doing that you will not only help us survive this famine, you can even help me go to the market, sell whatever we can lay our hands on, so we can at least feed. *Biko*, please, my child, try to understand. I know it won't be easy for you but I plead with you to reason with me," she said, her eyes misting with tears.

Convulsing in protest, Ijem screamed, "No, I reject this." If she was older she could have added; 'it's not my portion,' in line with today's Pentecostal lingo. With misty eyes she continued, "I have to continue my education. I want to go to school until I become a graduate. Nne, I need to finish school. Nne, please, don't stop me," she pleaded.

"Ijem, please try to understand. I really wish I could do otherwise," she pleaded with her grandchild.

"Nne, this is not a good one at all. This is bad news for a holiday. Nne, please, I will have to continue. I have only completed JSS 1. Ah, what will happen to me if I quit school at eleven? Nne, that was not our plan now? What will I be doing for the rest of my life? I must continue," she resolved, stamping her feet severally on the ground in protest, with tears streaming down her cheeks.

"Ijem, my daughter, insisting that you must continue with your education is tantamount to hanging your cloak beyond your reach. It will be very difficult to bring it down when you need it," she explained, gesticulating with her arms flailing above her head. "Please, my child, we cannot afford it now, and that is the bone of contention. Please, let's not build our castle in the air. I am not trying to stop you for stopping sake," Nnedimma further explained.

Still heaving her body vigorously in disagreement, Ijem argued, "No, Mama, I want to finish school. I am not hanging anything beyond my reach."

"Like I have already said, we need to cut our clothes according to our size, else it will either be too tight or too loose," Nnedimma interjected.

"I am only hoping on the God that brought me into this world to make a way for me. Nne, please don't stop me," Ijem said, as she knelt down and started sobbing again.

"My dear little girl, please try to understand the situation," Nnedimma kept pleading.

"No, Nne, providence will see me through my education. Please, let's not give up, Nne. He will make a way where there is no way. Please, Nne. Don't stop me, please. This is what my heart yearns for. I want to go to school, graduate and get a good job so I can take good care of you. Please, Nne, I will try my best. I will continue with the businesses that I do. That way I will make money for my school fees and also enough for our upkeep. I will do that every day before school resumes. I will intensify my *mkpa aki* and *ukpaka* search in the bush. I will gather enough *aki* and *ukpaka* for sale. We would make enough money from the sales, Nne," she said with some sense of conviction. She stared at Nnedimma, expecting her to just concur, and bring this whole issue to closure, but Nnedimma was rather gobsmacked at her determination that she could barely utter a word.

Ijem continued. "Nne, please, do not stop me. I understand everything. I know that if you had money, I won't lack, but you don't have and I must acknowledge that you have tried so much for me. God will keep you for me so that I can take care of you just the way you are taking good care of me. If I finish secondary school, and if I'm able to attend higher institution, Mama, our lives will forever be changed ... Nne!" she shook Nnedimma's legs.

"Eh, my daughter," she responded as if she had just woken up from a deep slumber.

"Do you know that I can be like that woman who visited the women's wing the other day when they held a meeting? I can be like her if I go to school. I can be seen on national television and then you can see me from anywhere you are. I will buy you a television. Connect our house to electricity. Nne, those things can only be achieved if I am educated," she preached to her grandmother enthusiastically.

"My daughter, all these things you said are good but the problem is that I don't have the money to pay your school fees. I did not go to school in my own time because my parents could not afford to pay my school fees."

Squatting down, Ijem asked her grandmother, "Nne, do you want me to sell oranges and groundnut for the rest of my life?"

"No, my daughter! How could you say a thing like that? Please, I want you to be among those *big big* people that they carry with *aromplane,*" her word for aeroplane. "I want those police crying motorcycles to follow you like they are following Obiageli" (a minister). She paused with a bit of regret in her voice. "But she is a daughter of a very wealthy man and they trained her in the best university in the country. *Nwam*, I really want the best for you. But it pains me that I don't have the capacity to give you the best," she sighed.

"Nne, I know you will if you can. Please, just help me the much you can. Please, let me continue. Please, Nne, that is all I ask of you, please"

Nnedimma wore a worried expression, as she reached out to wipe Ijem's tears. "My daughter, please, I don't want you to get involved in anything bad just to achieve this dream of yours." Ijem nodded and smiled.

Every morning, Ijem would hurry over her regular morning chores, such as sweeping and tidying up the compound, washing the dishes, packing the ashes from the previous day's cooking, warming the food and sometimes fetching water from the stream which she usually did in the evening. After these, she would either accompany her grandmother to the farm or take a small basket and set out visiting every palm tree in their neighbourhood in search of palm nuts. Sometimes, she would set herself a target; *I want to fill this basket before returning home.* This kind of target took her as far as their neighbouring villages, rummaging through the bushes. That way, she gathered a mound of palm kernels. Then she would start cracking them to extract the *aki*. This aspect actually took her a lot of time before she could crack a bucketful. Notwithstanding, she persevered because she was certain her grandmother would easily sell the palm kernels as well as the shell. What she did was lucrative because of its economic value; the palm kernel shell is used to pave roads and also used as fuel for cooking, the palm kernel oil is used for medicinal purposes, and for soap making. The palm kernel could be eaten with soaked garri. It could also be eaten with a popular food which Ndigbo love so much ... *ukwa*. The palm kernel can also be ground and mixed with flour along with other ingredients to bake various kinds of snacks. Most times, Ijem sustained blisters. Her grandmother treated her hands with warm water, salt and *okwuma*, shea butter. Nnedimma would sometimes help Ijem in cracking the palm nuts, although it usually increased the intensity of her sickness.

On the days Ijem did not go for *mkpa aki*, she went hunting for scattered *ukpaka*, oil bean seeds. In the night, she would go searching for snails. She continued these ventures and was able to haul in a half bagful of *aki*, two small buckets filled with *ukpaka* and a sizeable quantity of snail. Some of her snails unfortunately died probably due to starvation. The only way she could preserve the remnants was by putting in some green cassava leaves into the basket for them to feed on.

Nnedimma gathered Ijem's wares and sold them at Nkwo-Ikenga, a market located in a neighbouring town which held every four market days. She realised enough money to pay for Ijem's school fees. When the next school term began Ijem gladly resumed to continue with her JSS 2.

✡ ✡ ✡ ✡ ✡

One fateful day, during the JSS 2 third term holidays, Ijem set out for her usual hunting escapade but mistakenly stepped on a trap that was hidden for animals in the bush. It hurt her right leg so badly. She managed to free her leg from the iron trap and limped her way back home. She spent weeks writhing in pains. Nnedimma tended her wounds to the best of her knowledge; with very painful herbal leaves, warm salty water and *okwuma*. Ijem squirmed in pains for weeks before the wound healed. And it was only one month to school resumption and coincidentally when she had just turned twelve.

Nnedimma's heart continued to be broken each time she thought about her granddaughter's plight. "Ijem," she called again.

"Yes, Nne," Ijem answered unenthusiastically.

"See what has happened to you where you went scavenging the whole bushes in Afanasaa so we can raise money for your school fees. I feel very bad. My heart is heavy seeing you suffer this much, and yet doing very well in school. How long will this go on? How long can you take this? How many more wounds would you sustain before you complete your education? The other day, it was *agbala*, the itchy plant, that you contracted. You came back screaming and scratching your whole body. Now, it's a trap set for wild animals that caught you. Who knows what next? I am afraid," she sounded off.

"Nne, don't worry. I will be more careful this time," Ijem promised.

❧‖ *Two* ‖❧

Ijem's plight seemed not to have abated. It was midday when a girl's voice was again heard in the bush screaming and calling for help. Ijem was in trouble. Ujo, the palm wine tapper rushed in the direction of the sound only to find Ijem crying. She had just been bitten on the leg by a snake. Ujo pursued and killed the big snake that was about slithering away. He quickly removed his T-shirt and tied it tightly on her leg slightly above the point of the snake's bite; apparently to prevent the venom from spreading in her body. He cut and squeezed some fluid from some leaves allowing some of it to drop on the wound before taking her home. Again Nnedimma wept as soon she learnt of what had happened. Ijem's right leg was swollen. She was taken to a chemist's shop where she was treated.

Ihuoma, her aunty, paid for the drugs. Ihuoma was Nnedimma's second daughter who lived not far away from them. She was a seamstress.

Two weeks later, Nnedimma spoke to Ijem again concerning quitting school for good given the series of mishaps that had befallen her in recent times. Nnedimma and Ijem were seated on the mat on the pavement in front of the house. They needed air. Ijem sat up supporting her frame with both hands fixed on the mat. She was facing Nnedimma who sat hunched, inspecting Ijem's almost healed wound. Nnedimma started her conversation broaching an entirely new topic. "On a second thought, Ijem, I will advise you consider accepting one of your suitors for marriage since I can't afford footing the bill for your education, and God knows that I can't stand you hurting yourself any further."

"Nne, God forbid that I get married at this age! Nne, have you forgotten that I am just twelve?" she asked, narrowing her eyes in utter disbelief. "Nne, what are you saying? Nne, did you marry at my age or is it because I appear bigger than my mates? Hey, Mama! How could you even suggest that? I am sorry, Nne, but that is not an option." She folded her legs inwards as if to bring the conversation to a close and emphasise her unreadiness for such a venture, and then sat back leaning on the support of her left hand.

"*Nwa m*, I understand your feelings. I wish I had options to choose from. I wish I could do better than watch you hurt yourself to see yourself through school at your age. Although, I will be pleased to see my child become educated, I cannot afford it and I hate seeing you with all these injuries and scars. Look at your legs with all manner of bruises, a*pa, apa,* everywhere. I had always wished for my child to be educated. That was what I wished for your mother but circumstances did not permit that. Now, you have the potential to be anything you want to become if you get the right education, but I am helpless as it is. I can't afford your education especially for senior secondary. I learnt the school fees is higher than junior secondary." She turned to Ijem and held her closer. "My dear, try and consider picking one out of those eligible young men seeking your hand in marriage. I strongly feel you should accept one of them so that one of them as a husband can help us. The person may even see you through school," she pleaded. Ijem broke into a scowl and freed herself from her granny's bosom.

"How can I get married now, Nne? Nne you need not worry. I will use this holiday to do business with you. I can prepare your oil bean for sale and by the time I do that throughout the holidays we will have enough money for my school. That way, I will stop ransacking the bushes," Ijem pleaded.

"But it's not just about preparing the *ukpaka* that matters. What about the market to make the sales? You see, my child, *ukpaka* business has its season. It moves more during festive periods like Christmas when city people come home for Christmas. That's when they usually would want to eat roast yam with palm oil, *utazi* and *ugba*. Or during Asala festival, the festival which guarantees the mass return of our people every five years, or during the *iri ji,* that is the new yam festival. Apart from these periods in the year, the business moves very slowly. Preparing too much will get the *ugba* rotten and that is not a good way of doing business. You know *ugba* is perishable once prepared?" Ijem nodded. "That is the main problem, nwa m," Nnedimma explained.

Ijem exhaled deeply. "So, what do we do now, Mama? We have to think up another solution because I really need to continue school. Please, Nne," she urged, looking up at her.

Nnedimma looked at her for a while and turned away, supporting her jaw with her left hand as she thought again: *I have never seen somebody that loves education like this girl.* She turned to Ijem, and said, "My daughter, may the God that gave you shrew also give you the water to wash your hands." She paused and said again, "The only alternative may be to talk with Ihuoma, your aunty, and see if she could help you do any other less tedious business."

"Hmm, that is a great idea, Nne. How come we never thought of that? Nne, I will discuss with her when she returns in the evening."

"Okay, *nwa m.*" Ijem broke into a big smile. Nnedimma, stared at her grandchild in deep admiration but shook her head at what the little girl was passing through. *O Chim!* she thought, looking up to the sky. Stretching her thoughts, she focused on her past. *I thought this little girl's case would be different from mine and her mother's. Why must she suffer like I have been suffering all my life?*

Nnedimma in her lifetime as a woman had really bitten more than her own fair share of suffering.

Nnedimma grew up knowing nothing but difficulty. Her father was a farmer and all his children did nothing else but farm. Proceeds from the farm were barely enough to feed the large household which comprised many children and wives. Nnedimma was married off to her husband without her own consent. Her consent was not important, and to her, it was a relief being married off to another household where she queued up alongside other wives to compete and crave attention from her husband. She grew up from a father who had no time for her or any of his numerous children. The little attention she had came from her own mother who was one of the numerous wives of her father. Getting married was some kind of elixir even though her consent was not sought. The attention and love she was looking for was never to be. She got married into a hostile family where her co-wives saw themselves as sworn enemies. Her suffering got even worse after she lost her husband a few years into the marriage. Her children came in quick successions. She had five children: Ihuoma, Nneka, Chuka, Emeka and Chiazo. Her quest for a female child whom she believed would take care of her in old age resulted in the last two boys before she gave up trying– Emeka and Chiazo in that order. In her old age she was now living in penury and grappling with the uncommon demands of a grand-daughter whom she so much adored.

Snapping out of her reverie, she thought aloud: *Why can't things just be different for this little girl? Why do I have such a hard luck?* Redirecting her attention to Ijem, she wiped her cheek with the back of her palms, and then said, "Don't worry, my child, the

God that brought you to me will provide for us. He will take care of our needs, especially your much desired education," she tailed off.

"Yes, Mama," Ijem muttered smiling as she placed her left palm on her grandmother's. "We will be fine, Nne," the little girl said smiling brightly.

Feeling a lot better, both diverted their attention to the livestock. "That goat looks pregnant," Nnedimma said, standing up to get a closer look at the goat. "Ijem, when last did we bring an *mkpi* to mate these goats?" Nnedimma asked.

"Mama, it was about three months ago. I can remember, it was that week we did confirmation in the church. I brought the *mkpi* that Saturday before leaving for catechism," Ijem explained.

"But I asked Ekemma to release her *mkpi* to these goats last two Eke market days?"

"No, Nne, I didn't see any."

"Okay then, please, run to Ekemma's house now and tell her to please allow you bring her *mkpi* for these goats," Nnedimma instructed.

"Okay, Nne," she said and she ran out. Shortly after, she returned holding the leash that was tied to the goat to prevent it from running away. She only released the rope when she got into their compound. Immediately, the he-goat started its funny routine; bleating in its peculiar manner while running after the she-goats. Ijem and her granny watched awhile without both saying anything.

"Ehn, Nne, what are we preparing for dinner? It's getting late, look at the shadow," Ijem said, pointing at her already elongated shadow. "Hmm. There is no food in this house," she said, alerting her grandmother. "*Achicha* remains the only option."(*Achicha* is sun-dried plantain strips. During the plantain season, as a way of preserving it for the famine season, commonly referred to as *ugani,* unripe plantain is boiled with its back peeled, and diced in circles and thereafter sun-dried. Each time it was needed, some would be pounded to the desired sizes and can be boiled alone or with yam, beans, or vegetable.)

"*Ngwa nu,* go and bring down the *achicha* bag, and get the mortar ready. I will join you shortly," Nnedimma instructed. Ijem did as she was directed. She squatted in the kitchen beside the mortar, holding the pestle in readiness. When Nnedimma joined her and measured a plateful of *achicha* into the mortar, she asked her to start pounding it. "Make sure you do not overpound it. Don't turn it into powder," she warned, holding her right ear.

"I know how to pound it, Nne."

"I'm just reminding you even though I trust your judgement. Again, when you are done, set the firewood and bring out the small *ite-igwe,* while I go and fetch *onugbu,*" Nnedimma said as she bounded out to the garden to fetch the bitter leaf. *Onugbu* serves as vegetable for cooking especially when the regular u*gu* or *bologi* are out of season. *Bologi* is a West African perennial climbing plant that is used as a potherb. It is usually supported by a stake or trellised. It is cultivated mainly under a shade and propagated by pruning because it keeps on blossoming. The fruits also serve as food.

It was late in the evening when Ihuoma returned from her tailoring business. She was having her dinner and Ijem who had been lurking and following her around looking for the best way to put her request through, called out, "Aunty!"

"What is it, Ijem? Are you okay? You look worried," Ihuoma said, with a mouthful of *achicha* in her mouth.

"Aunty, yes. I need your help."

Ihuoma eyed her little niece again, wondering. "How do you mean? Are you hungry?" she asked in a barrage.

"No, Aunty. You said you knew how to prepare boiled

groundnuts the other day?" Ijem pointedly reminded her aunty, looking at her as if to force out an affirmative answer.

"Yes, Ijem," came her aunt's cheery response. "Come and sit down here. What is it with boiled groundnuts? Do you want to eat some groundnuts?" Without waiting for her response, she promised to get her some. "Don't worry, I will buy you some tomorrow when I go to the market."

"No, Aunty, I want to sell the groundnuts. I want to do groundnut business."

Ihuoma could not believe her ears. "You," she said, pointing at Ijem, "want to sell groundnuts?"

"Yes, Aunty. I need to raise some money for my school fees before school resumes. Please, I need your help," Ijem said, sounding desperate.

"Hmm!" Ihuoma heaved, looking at the little girl with so much compassion. "*Chai!*" she exclaimed. "Has it come to this? This life! If it wasn't for this operation that I just had that took all my savings, I would have at least paid for one term for you, my little amazing girl. Now I'm not even strong enough to sew clothes yet. I only go out at the moment just for people who want to collect the clothes that I have already made. I'm not to pedal the machine in the next three to four months, as the doctor instructed," she said regrettably.

"My dear, nevertheless, I will arrange to get half bag of groundnuts for a start. I will talk to Mama Beatie to see if I can convince her to release at least half bag of groundnuts to us. We would pay her as the sales proceed."

"Thank you, Aunty. God bless you," Ijem said effusively.

"God bless you too, my dear little girl," Ihuoma said as she watched Ijem walk out of the room. Ihuoma shook her head in amazement. *This girl is just too wise for her age*, she thought.

"Buy groundnuts! Buy groundnuts!" Ijem kept shouting as she

walked about the market. Before midday, she had finished selling the first bucket. She ran to her aunt's shop and rendered account of her business. It was great. She made some profit. Selling groundnuts became a routine for Ijem throughout the holidays after her morning chores. Her aunty kept the profit for her while she used the rest to pay for the credit facility.

Each evening, after the day's business, Ijem would run home to do her evening chores. Nnedimma also helped out as much as her illness would permit but left Ijem to contend with the chore of going to the stream. Most times, she would do several trips so that they would have enough water to last till the following evening.

Going to the stream for Ijem was interesting especially when going with a lot of other kids. Even though it involved walking a long distance characterised by a steep and a bumpy path. It was fun going as it meant running down the bumpy but steep path even though sometimes some of them would fall and get hurt; because when they do so they roll, scraping and bruising their body. But the harder and boring part was going home with a water pot placed on the head and walking unsteadily on the jagged pathway. For someone like Ijem, there was no alternative. On Saturdays, she would gather all their dirty clothes, fold them in one wrapper and tie it to her back, pick up her keg and run to the stream. She would wash the clothes, and dry them in the sun. The fun part was usually the intervening period which she used to play with the other children in the stream while waiting for her clothes to dry. The Saturday trip was usually the longest and most tedious. Most times, she would stop on her way home, open her keg and pour some water on herself for invigoration as this helped her to enjoy the walk back home under the scorching sun.

❦❙ *Three* ❙❦

Ijem's doggedness would not let her relent. Her commitment, determination and love for education would equally not flag. She always thought about how to make more money to augment her school fees. One day, on her way to the market, she saw a man standing by a heap of sand while people came hauling away some bags apparently filled with sand. She saw money exchange hands and was excited at the huge amount the buyers paid the sand owner. *"Chei!"* she screamed silently. She placed her hand over her opened mouth. *Look at all that money,* she thought again. She made up her mind and told herself. *I will start piling some sand come next rainy season.*

A day to resumption, Ijem washed her uniform and ironed it with a charcoal iron. The next day, she gladly resumed school with her mates. The school infrastructure was in a decrepit state. The classrooms had most of its louvres either missing or half-broken. One side of the entrance door had fallen off, which left the classroom open just like every other classroom in the school. In the middle of the wall facing the class was a darkened patch which served as the blackboard. Some students were standing, while others were seated on makeshift stools, chairs and whatever they could lay their hands on. They were various groups clustered around a storyteller. Those students who spent their holidays in the cities came to school with something new; either a wristwatch, schoolbag, sandal, snack or anything Ijem considered strange or would she rather say, alien to the village. Other students gathered to admire the new things or to get a pinch of whatever edible they brought to school. The holiday makers told many interesting stories. Those who went to Lagos told similar stories about the Bar Beach, Lekki Beach, the flyovers across the lagoon, the pedestrian bridges, Third Mainland Bridge and so on. Those who went to Abuja, told stories about Aso Rock, the various parks, the beautiful roads, and the airport. These stories made those who had no new stories to tell, like Ijem, look and feel very odd.

Seizing the opportunity of their awkwardness, Chinenye said to Ijem, "Is it not clear that we have planted bottles, and it's only the day the bottles germinate, that we would leave this village for holidays in the city?"

Ijem agreeing with her said, "Abi, I pray they germinate soon because I'll like to go to the city and see things for myself." Continuing, she said, "They said they have gigantic buildings that reach heaven in Lagos."

"Are you serious?" asked Chinenye, obviously stunned. "Hmm, that means that the people who live up there in those buildings will be seeing God every day," she added.

"They are neighbours with God," Ijem said, adding, "I can't wait to see such buildings."

"One day is one day, monkey will go to the market," Chinenye enthused. They both laughed.

"Who is the monkey? You?" Ijem asked, pointing at Chinenye.

"Please, I am not in the monkey league," Chinenye said jokingly.

Out of her savings, the one she made during the holidays, Ijem paid her school fees promptly without being sent out of school. The money she made from the groundnut sales was enough to pay her school fees for the first term. During the second term which coincided with the rainy season, she started gathering sand whenever it rained. She blocked drainages with stones and whatever she could lay her hands on so that some sand would be lodged at those points as the water drained off when it rained. Before the end of the holidays all her small heaps at various points amounted to two tipper trips of sand. She asked her grandmother to make the sales for her but Nnedimma declined, saying: "We would sell them during the dry season, by then, it will fetch us more money."

"Okay, Mama, you know better," Ijem said, agreeing with the suggestion her granny had made.

"My daughter, do you know, sometimes, I wonder if you are a female or a male child. You are not feeble like girls of your age. You are strong-willed; and so determined. I am so grateful to God for bringing you to me. For giving me a complete bundle of joy. You are *agu be m,* my lioness. You baffle me with your approach to issues. How many girls of your age can do what you do? You help me in the farm, you cook, you go to the stream, you do every house chore there is to be done, you sell groundnuts, you gather sand. Ah-ah! Only you? You are my strength, Ijem." Ijem smiled as Nnedimma lavished all that praise on her.

They hugged and suddenly Ijem looked at her grandmother with a grim face and launched into a little speech. Some sort of appreciation and reassurance. "Mama, I will stop at nothing to make you happy. I will not let you do much work again because I don't want you to fall ill again. When I make enough money, I will take you to the hospital where they will permanently cure this sickness that is always disturbing you, okay?" Nnedimma smiled. And both of them laughed heartily, exhilarated and feeling quite good with themselves.

Nnedimma sold the heaps of sand around December, and with the proceeds Ijem was able to register for her Junior Secondary School Examinations. She would study every evening when she returned from school which was quite some distance from the house. The school was located in Afaani, three villages away from her grandmother's village, Afaenu. She walked for a minimum of one hour to school every morning. Sometimes if she trotted, the time could be reduced to a forty-five minute journey.

Her evening routine was: fetching fodder for the goats, preparing dinner, if it was during the rainy season, she would usually fetch water from their neighbours who had a well for water storage. Sometimes, they would turn her down, especially during the dry season.

On Saturdays during the dry season, she would go to the farm to clear the bush for the forthcoming farming season; she would go for *ikpa ji*, searching for forgotten and unharvested yams in people's farms. Amidst all these, Ijem still found time to read and prepare for her examinations. Soon, the examination came and passed. It ushered in the longest holidays in her school life. Three months long.

She was thirteen. Her industrious nature kept suitors trailing her. As they kept showing up, Nnedimma at some point gave the idea a serious thought. *Hmm, the way suitors are coming for Ijem, I think it is her destiny to get married early. This may be the sign that her husband is meant to come at this age and not when she is older. But the problem is that she doesn't even want to hear anybody discuss this sort of issue.* With these thoughts on her mind, Nnedimma tried once again, urging Ijem to pick a husband out of the increasing suitors.

"Nne, there you go again. Please, must we go over this every time? Please, Nne. I am not ready to get married. What is on my mind at the moment is how to intensify my groundnut business. It is the season again. I hope to make enough for my school fees within this holiday period. I'll want to go to senior college."

This time, she sold groundnuts combined with other things. She would follow the boys to pluck mangoes, from and around the leprosy centre. They would sneak into the compound through a fence; the boys would help her climb over the fence either by supporting her with their hands on her buttocks or dragging her across the fence. They would share the proceeds of what they were able to pluck from the mango trees and each person would determine what to do with his or her share. Ijem sold hers at the junction, especially to passengers who stopped by the highway. Apart from hawking groundnuts and mangoes, she joined the boys in her area to sand-fill some potholes on the highway for the meagre amounts it pleased the road users to drop for them. At the end of the day, they would share the money they realised. These were what preoccupied Ijem throughout the holidays rather than considering lecherous men who wanted a baby girl to snatch from the cradle. She was certain she would have enough money to pay for her school fees, and was looking forward to being addressed as a senior by the junior students.

Nnedimma took Ijem to Nkwo-Ikenga market so she could buy a new school uniform material for her since the senior students' style was slightly different from that of the juniors.

Ijem returned home from the market happy, and eagerly awaited the school resumption day to come. Ihuoma, her aunty, made the uniform for her. But Ijem's tall dream came crashing on a Friday night of the last weekend to school resumption. Her grandmother had yet another bout of attack. She could not breathe normally. Her breath was heavy and wheezy. One could hear the wheezy sound of her breath from the neighbours. Nnedimma stretched herself in a bid to create airways to her lungs. Her lungs were inflamed. She was basically 'walking on her head' that night. It was so bad that nobody slept in the house. Ihuoma managed to carry Nnedimma in a wheel barrow to the nearby health centre. The doctor demanded a deposit before beginning the treatment for her. Lo and behold there was nowhere to raise the money other than from Ijem's savings for her school fees. Ihuoma dipped her hands into her own savings but it was not enough. They took part of Ijem's money to pay for the deposit. "She is asthmatic," said the doctor. Ijem and Ihuoma looked confused over the disclosure.

"Doctor what do you mean by a-zma...?" queried the completely petrified Ijem.

The doctor explained. "It is an allergy. It can only be managed for now. The only thing here is that she should avoid strenuous tasks, dusty environments, smoke or anything that can choke her," he advised.

"But, Doctor, you should give her drugs now to cure it," Ijem suggested. Continuing she told the doctor to cure her grandmother from this illness because there was no way she could avoid dust and smoke.

"Our roof is open. Dust and smoke freely come into the room," Ihuoma further added, confirming what her niece had just told the doctor.

"I have heard what you people have said. It can only be managed. There's no cure that is what I am trying to say. The drugs we have now can only manage but not cure the ailment," the doctor insisted.

On Wednesday evening, when Nnedimma was being discharged, Ijem had no option than to complete the payment for her drugs, and then for the inhaler which the doctor had insisted they buy, harping on what good it would do to alleviate Nnedimma's breathing difficulty. With that expense, that was how her whole savings evaporated!

Ijem could not resume school with her mates that week primarily because she was taking care of her sick grandmother.

Besides that, there was no need for her to have gone to school at all when her fees had not been paid.

God! What am I going to do now? How will I go back to school? How do I pay my fees now?

She prayed and slept off. One week passed, Ijem went about her normal business but with uncertainty regarding her further education. She thought, *the only option I have now is to skip the term and use the period to do more business so I can raise money for my school fees for next term. Hmm, but then, that would mean skipping a whole term. How will I catch up? Besides, the school may not even admit me for the second term without showing them a report card for the first term. What do I do now?* She relapsed into a very pensive mood, with her head throbbing. Sometimes she became bemused, and most times unhappy.

On Sunday, she went to church, Our Lady's Catholic Church, Afanasaa. During the period for announcements, after the boring sermon which she did not pay much attention to, Ijem jumped up so high from her seat when she heard the announcement that, "The state government has declared free education for all the secondary schools in the state, effective September." Ijem sang through her way home, praising God for the miracle, chanting:

ihe nile banyerem n'emetu chukwu n'obi,
echiche udo, oganiru k'onechere mo o,
ogaghi ekwe ka echiche ndi iro mezue,
amara chineke, bara uba n'ebe m no.

All my concerns bother the Lord.
Thoughts of peace and progress He has for me.
He will render futile the plans of the enemies.
God's grace is sufficient for me.

$\circledcirc\|$ *Four* $\|\circledcirc$

The first term of Senior Secondary (SS1) was very exciting for many students, especially those in Ijem's class because of the fact that they were now being addressed as seniors. Junior students according to the school's tradition appended the word, 'senior' to their names in reverence. And more so because of the difference in their uniforms. And then for the funny reason that whenever the junior students wanted to come into the classroom of the seniors they would take permission. For this reason alone, some senior students deliberately invited the junior students to their classes just to relish the fact that the junior students would stand at the door of the senior class, with their right hand raised and say the words: "Excuse me, seniors, please, may I come in?"

The response would usually be: "Repeat", "jump in", "crawl in", and so on. The response varied depending on the mood of the person who saw the junior approaching the entrance of the classroom.

Ijem was particularly happy that she was able to return to school. She always paid close attention to teachers as if she wanted to learn everything at once because she entertained the fear that she may be asked to drop out of school again.

Again, she dreaded the suggestion: "You may have to consider one of your suitors." At the moment in her school, there were no teachers for mathematics, french and agriculture. The vacancies were filled by 'corpers' as they were commonly called. 'Corpers' referred to fresh graduates from the universities carrying out their compulsory one-year National Youth Service Corps (NYSC) programme. The mathematics teacher was quite good. His classes were interesting. Ijem was so inspired to give in her best that after attending a few mathematics classes, she borrowed her classmate's mathematics textbook on a weekend and attempted solving all exercises on the topic the teacher taught. The next Monday, she took her answers to the mathematics teacher to mark. The teacher was impressed. That singular act aroused his interest in Ijem.

Occasionally, he would have a chat with her if they bumped into each other. The 'corper' fondly called Ola, a short form of his name Olatoyinbo, told Ijem, "You are a covenant child. Always remember this. You will go places and God's grace is upon you."

The service year came to an end, Ola and other 'corpers' were bid farewell with a send-off party organised by the students. They bought gifts for their departing teachers.

The send-off party coincided with the beginning of a year-long teachers' strike in the state. The state government had suddenly revoked the free education policy they had promulgated because, according to what Ijem had heard, the state government had become bankrupt and as a result could not pay the teachers their salaries and allowances because of the loss of revenue it used to generate from the school fees.

The teachers at first started a sit-down strike; the teachers would be in school but would not teach. Neither would they attend to the students nor participate in any other academic exercise. Two months into that 'work-to-rule action', they embarked on a full strike due to the non-payment of their salaries by the government, giving the excuse that the teachers had not worked to earn the pay.

The state government in a bid to reopen the closed schools came up with a rather ridiculous huge school fees, and mandated that the terms that had been spent at home would also be paid for. That meant that each student would pay school fees for three terms at once. This resulted in a state-wide riot. There was destruction of school properties in some schools especially the boys' schools. Ijem was left with no option than to stay at home. She intensified efforts on her businesses and immersed herself in her grandmother's business so as to raise the money for her granny's drugs and their feeding.

Meanwhile suitors kept on coming in droves. Some mothers and fathers in the village were trying to hook their sons to marry Ijem because of what they had observed about her conduct, good character and industriousness.

One Christmas during the strike, Ijem's uncles returned for holidays. There were only two rooms in their mud house. Ijem shared one of the rooms with her grandmother. The other one was taken up by her uncles. The eldest son, Emeka, was married and so slept in the sitting room with his wife.

Emeka, who was living in Lagos, had no job and was practically doing nothing. According to the story that Ijem heard, he was said to have served a ritualist during his apprenticeship. As is consistent with such characters, his master was rumoured to have mysteriously taken back the money which he used in setting him up after his apprenticeship. He even invoked a kind of uselessness on him, purportedly for his own gain. To the extent that it was said that as long as Emeka remained useless, his master prospered. How plausible that is remained debatable. So, Emeka and her other uncles coming home for holidays added no value for Ijem and her grandmother.

On December twenty-sixth of that year, they held a family meeting. Emeka and Chiazo sat on a bench while Nnedimma and Ijem sat on an *okpoga*. Without disguising his discomfiture, Emeka told Ijem, "I strongly think you should get married. You have come of age now and I heard you already have many suitors ..."

Impatiently, Ijem shot back at him. "I am not getting married now, Uncle. I have not finished school!"

"And who said that finishing school is a prerequisite for

getting married?" he queried in anger. "You should do well and just get married. Marry one of those men so that you can vacate the room for us. We do not have enough space in this house, and you are here occupying the available one when you have the option of getting married. It's not as if there is money to send you to school. Why would you prefer to be stupid about making up your mind? Why the wait? You are big enough for marriage," he roared.

Chiazo, Ijem's other uncle who was getting by, doing menial jobs and carpentry work added his own voice. "Ijem, please just accept to marry one of these men and things will be better for us. The man may even help us. Just get married. I don't know why you are so obsessed with this school thing. Just get married. Even the state government has shut down all the secondary schools in the state, so why are you still bothered about going to school?"

Without another word, Ijem got up and left the meeting. She was dismayed. The ongoing episode reminded her once again that she did not really belong there. She found a corner in the compound and wept bitterly. She cried to heaven for help. The thought of getting married at fourteen gave her goose pimples. She did not eat for the rest of the day. She continued sobbing until she slept off at night.

"Ijem, wake up, let's talk," Nnedimma said while shaking Ijem up to rouse her from sleep. Nnedimma who sat through the meeting and watched what had transpired was disturbed. It was about 3.00 am on December 27. Ijem wiped sleep off her eyes, and asked her grandmother sleepily.

"Nne, is everything alright?"

"Ijem, my daughter, I am afraid," her grandmother answered tentatively. Continuing, she said, "I don't want anything to happen to you. You have had about seven serious suitors within two years. I strongly feel you should marry one of them."

"Nne, what is it again this night? I don't want to listen anymore to this husband talk, Mama, please," Ijem said wearing a long face.

"No, my daughter. I am not doing this to hurt you. No! Rather it's for your own good. Ijem, please. I am no longer strong. Nobody knows what tomorrow holds for me due to my health situation. Nwa m, please, consider getting married seriously. You have come of age. Besides, there is no money to send you to school. I don't want you to keep suffering like this. I want a man to take care of you for me. Your uncles, my sons will all soon get married, and I don't want their wives to maltreat you when I am no longer there. My dear, please think about this. I need you to do this for me. I won't deceive you," she preached.

Tears began to flow freely again. Ijem's face was covered with rivulets of tears running down her cheeks like a flowing stream. "Nne, is this the only option for me? Is getting married the solution to our problems? Oh God!" she cried even more.

"My dear, think about it, look through the ranks of all your uncles. Who or which one of them is there to help you? Nobody! They need help themselves. So, you see my child, I think it's the right time. Again, you started having suitors quite young. It may be an indication that you are destined to marry very young." She kept on pressing.

Ijem was vehement. "Nne, I don't want to get married now. How will my classmates look at me?"

"Which classmates?" Nnedimma retorted, adding quickly, "What about Ifeoma, the daughter of Nkoli Obi, didn't she get married last year? Is she not in your school? Go and see her mother now. She is always adorning big *Hollandaise* from her in-law."

"Ehn! Nne? What about Amara that got married to one man I don't know? Look at her today. She looks older than you, Nne. She hawks oranges and wears tattered clothes."

"Forget Amara," Nnedimma interrupted her waving her right hand in dismissal. "Your destiny is different. Yours will be better.

My daughter, get back to sleep. We'll talk more in the morning. We'd better talk when you can comprehend. *Kachifo*." Nnedimma sat back and watched as Ijem refused to lie down again. She could no longer sleep. Instead she resumed crying.

The rest of the Christmas period was bad for Ijem. She did not show up at the events that usually took place during the Christmas period such as the church organised bazaar, football matches, masquerade parade and so on. She brooded and was so depressed and pale. She fell ill after some days. She was given pain relieving tablets which reduced her temperature.

She woke up one morning and refused to get up from her mat. Nnedimma went into the room and sat by her on the mat, holding her close and pleading with her. "Ijem, look at what you are doing to yourself. You are breaking my heart. Please, stop starving yourself. I will never deceive you." Ijem buried her head and cried in her bosom.

After crying for awhile, Ijem broke away from her grandmother and pointedly asked, "Nne, why is it that nobody wants to support me in my quest for education? Why is everybody pushing me to marry? Nne, is this fair?"

Nnedimma admonished her to stop crying. She was interrupted by Egodi, her neighbour, who had stopped by to call her to join them for the *Inyomoha* meeting, an association of women. Nnedimma quickly tied her head scarf and left the compound with Egodi.

Ijem got up, paced about the untidy compound. Walking a few paces, she walked towards the huge tree and sat on one of the surface roots of the *ugiri* tree. As if in a trance, she drifted off reflecting on who she was, and the journey of her life so far …

❦‖ *Five* ‖❦

It had started in a small town called Afanasaa. An obscure rusty town located in the south-eastern part of Nigeria. It was a misty cold harmattan morning. The weather was comforting for the privileged who could afford the comfort and warmth of their duvets or blankets. Unlike some children who had no such privileges.

Ijem, a seven-year-old, was one of such children. As she emerged from the kitchen, wrapped up in an old and torn piece of woolen clothes, shivering, she painted a picture of a starry-eyed and a frightened child emerging from a hole after a bomb blast. She was shivering not only as a result of the terribly cold weather, but because of the utmost fear she felt about the usual vituperation that came from the man she called father. As she walked uncertainly, her steps unsure, she was going to ask him for money for her school report card. Kneeling in respect before her father, she greeted him: "Good morning, Papa." Enuma turned in her direction and looked her over in anger.

"Yes, what is it this morning? Why have you sworn that I will not drink and drop the cup in this house? What is it?" Raising his brows, he stretched his right hand as if he was expecting to receive something from her. "Speak before I lose my temper!" he yelled.

With a shaky voice Ijem muttered, "Papa, the headmaster forbids us coming to school today if we do not come along with the fifteen naira for the school report card."

"Is that so?" Enuma sneered. "That is your own cup of tea,"

Enuma snapped. "Did you hear me?" She nodded as she trembled in fear. "I said that's your absolute business. Just leave me out of this. If the headmaster said you should stay at home, then pick up your hoe and cutlass and go to the farm. I don't even know the essence of wasting time and money on you. What am I going to gain from spending any kobo on you? *Mtchew!*" he hissed.

He drew a long sigh and sat on his rickety couch as he reached for his snuff box tucked in one of his pockets. He held the box with his right hand and tapped it with the other hand, opened and poured some powdered tobacco in his left palm. He used the back of his thumb nail of the right hand to scoop and ferry it to his now dilated nostrils to sniff. His eyes turned reddish as he continued snorting. Looking up, he bawled, "What are you still doing here, you rat? Get out of my sight before you regret waking up this morning." He glared at her as she ran out of his sight, in tears. "Nonsense!" he added as he went back to his unfinished business.

The poor girl ran back into the kitchen and started crying. Nneka, a young woman in her early twenties, Ijem's mother and Enuma's wife, went to pacify her little daughter.

Nneka, a brown-skinned, shapely young woman with bright attractive pair of eyes that had considerably dimmed due to her frequent shedding of tears, and unhappiness drew her daughter closer to herself. Nneka's height was about 5 feet 7 inches with a beautiful set of white teeth which remained clenched and unopened most of the time because of the scowling countenance she'd adopted to checkmate Enuma's ranting and vituperations against her daughter and herself. She exploded when she heard her daughter crying. Shouting and cursing, she'd convulsed, shaking her body while holding her daughter tightly to her body. The body that was shaking was covered in some dowdy apparel. She had a graceful figure. An elegant figure that attracted Chris to her. That figure was no longer conspicuous due to poverty and maltreatment. She wore a gaunt and haggard look. She had only scruffy wears, mostly wrappers. These were clothes she had before she got married to Enuma.

There had never been a replacement, rather most of them had been patched up at different places. Although she was a very kind and humble young woman, she was a victim of circumstances. As a fourteen-year-old student of Girls' Secondary School, Afaani in Afanasaa, she had a horrible experience which no young woman, not to talk of a young girl of her age would wish her enemy to have. The story she never liked to remember. She would rather not tell it to anyone, not even Ijem.

Still in her reverie, she remembered that fateful Monday morning. As a diligent student on duty, Nneka arrived her school premises earlier than every other student. The school premises was unusually calm that she could feel her shadow walking behind her. The kind of tranquility that made her afraid at first. Covered in goose bumps she shivered at intervals as if hit by chills. Despite that she still had the presence of mind to admire the serenity of the academic environment as she walked toward the Introductory Technology (Intro Tech) laboratory. She stretched her thoughts and imagined what a sharp contrast the picture she just saw now could be when compared to what it would be within the next hour. She cast a few glances at the strutting and the variations in sizes and colours of the cockerels and hens that gathered far down the school field as she walked past. She wondered. Were the birds having a kind of meeting or were they observing their own version of morning devotion? The only thing that reminded her of the presence of other people in the compound was the faint but perceptible voices of girls who were jabbering away from the school dormitory at the far east of the school. She got to the lab and tried to hurry over her duties which included darkening the blackboard with a mixture of powdered charcoal and water, and the sweeping of the lab.

✻ ✻ ✻ ✻ ✻

She resented the memory that it was indeed inside that laboratory where she had been tidying up that her destiny was re-written. "Hello, Student," came the unsettling and unfamiliar voice. Nneka jumped in fright, apparently startled. She focused, narrowing her eyes and staring toward the direction where the voice had come from. Drawing closer from the south door of the lab, he'd asked somewhat politely, "May I know your name?"

"N-ne-ka Obi-di," she had stammered with a frightened and trembling voice.

"Hmm! Nice name for a beautiful girl …What class are you in?" he'd inquired further as he walked closer to her.

Nneka seeing that he was dressed in a corps member's uniform responded timidly, "JSS 3, Sir."

"Ok, ehm, I need your help before assembly starts. I need you to take those cartons of scripts and books to somewhere I will show you outside the school. You'll also help me to bring the ones that I have marked back to school. He said in a voice that was firm and assertive.

"Yes, Sir," she obediently agreed. She quickly rounded off her chores in the lab, rinsed her hands and wiped them on her blue pinafore uniform.

Her white belt loosened and fell off from her waist as she bent over to lift the carton. She dropped the carton, picked up her belt and fastened it tightly around her curvaceous waist. Chris watched in veiled admiration. She lifted the carton and gently placed it on her head, supporting it with her left hand and carried the other bag on the right hand. He led the way while she calmly followed to the school gate. When they passed the mango junction after the school gate, he slowed to walk beside her, and sometimes a little behind her. He swallowed hard as he watched her walk with a spectacular but timid elegance. She was a beauty, with statuesque-like formation. Everything about her was set in the proper place and right dimensions. To the extent that heads turned in utter admiration. Men always turned whenever she walked past them. As both of them walked along, Chris painted a mental picture of how this goddess would look beneath the school uniform. He was so lost in thoughts that they almost passed their destination.

It was a newly built but unpainted house which was owned by one of the rich men in Afanasaa, an absentee landlord who lived in Onitsha. The landlord had let out the boys' quarters of the building for Youth Corps members. Chris occupied one of the rooms in the detached bungalow behind the new house. He dipped his right hand in his right pocket for the door keys. He brought out a bunch of keys, searched for the right key to his room.

Nneka, who was still standing behind him carrying the carton of books, asked, "Sir, should I drop them here?" pointing at a corner of the pavement.

"No, no, no, hold on a little," Chris had said quickly. He opened the door, entered and then beckoned on her to come in. Nneka, an unassuming young girl, stepped into the room still carrying the carton and looking at him to show her where to drop them.

It was almost a regular student's room. There was an old foam dumped at the left corner of the room. A standing fan skewed downward facing the foam, a wooden hanger holding few clothes above where the fan stood, a wooden chair and a table at the right sitting close to the window. Under the table were some scattered scripts and papers.

"Please, keep them there," he instructed Nneka, gesturing at the far right corner of the room where he had stacks of scattered books. She hurriedly dropped the bag and lowered the carton to the uncarpeted floor.

She turned to leave only to find Chris right before her with his hands thrown wide apart as if beckoning her for an embrace. She shot frightened looks at the man blocking her and then at the door. The door had been locked. "Give me a hug, Angel, hug me, beautiful damsel, hug me, Omalicha, hug me, the goddess of beauty," he kept saying. Nneka confused and engulfed in fear reached for the door but was swept off her feet by the emotionally enraged Chris. Without warning, he ripped off her pinafore as she struggled to free herself from his strong grip. He hit her severally to quieten her as she struggled. It was pointless. He had covered her mouth with one hand and used his other hand and his knees to demobilize her. Her strength was not a match to his ...

After the ordeal, she wept all day and was so ashamed to return to school. *How can I go home today and what will I tell Aunty?* she asked in soliloquy thinking about the explanation she would give to her guardian, Mrs Obi. She was all messed up. Her uniform had blood stains. A few hours ago she had been a virgin. She didn't know how to explain what had just happened to her to her guardian. She suspected she would never believe her, not to talk of helping her. She sneaked into the house at night. Six weeks later, Mrs Obi discovered that she was pregnant. She beat her mercilessly, called her names and threw her out of her house. Mrs Obi went about town broadcasting that Nneka was a prostitute who had been pretending to be a virgin.

$\approx\|$ *Six* $\|\approx$

Nneka returned to her poor mother, dejected. Her mother, Nnedimma wept in disappointment, despair and desolation. She asked, *God, why me? Why my daughter, why us? What am I going to do? Who do I run to?* She wept and brooded the whole day. Nneka, on the other hand fell into depression and continued to wear a very gloomy outlook. It was a very difficult time in her life. She was so ashamed to go to school and report the case to the principal. One of her uncles, Pat, whom they fondly called Patty accompanied her, along with her mother to school to report the matter. To their utter shock and embarrassment, the principal treated the matter with levity, saying, "It's quite unfortunate!" adding, "I'm afraid, Madam, my record does not show any Youth Corps member named Chris among the batch of corps members who have just passed out. Sadly too," he said, with a smirk playing at the corner of his mouth, "the Corps members who passed out this previous week have all gone home, travelled out of town to different destinations. I'm afraid ..." he said, leaving the dejected uncle, mother and daughter to make up their minds about what to do with the matter.

Nneka cried her heart out when it dawned on her that 'Chris' might not have been the real identity of the Corps member that defiled her and got her pregnant.

✵　　✵　　✵　　✵　　✵

She became the object of ridicule. The villagers scorned her. She felt so bad, perceiving herself as a huge disappointment, not only to her family but also to the girls' guild, an association of the church to which she belonged. Soon, she stopped going to the market, attending church services, and even going to any public place.

She confined herself to her mother's hut, and each time a visitor came, she would hide having cautioned her mother to say that she was out assuming anyone asked.

She was full of regrets to the point that she attempted committing suicide. But then, she reneged considering the religious implication of killing herself given her Christian background. Nnedimma stood by her. She was her rock of Gibraltar. At any opportunity she would talk to her, even at midnight.

"My daughter, I understand how bad you may be feeling now. But I don't mind anymore. Since we could not find the man who is responsible, let's do this together. I am no longer disappointed as I was at first, having heard the story of how it happened. Please, be strong, carry this pregnancy to its full term and deliver the child for me. I will take the child from you upon delivery so you can join your fellow girls again," she assured her.

After series of ill-motivated advice and attempts to have her terminate the pregnancy by her friends, Nneka pondered over and over on the repercussion of terminating the pregnancy, and decided against it. With her mother's constant encouragement, she gradually developed a positive disposition. In no time, she agreed to keep the pregnancy damning the consequences. Nine months gone, Nneka was delivered of a pretty baby girl whom her mother thoughtfully named Ijeabalum, translated literally to mean a rewarding venture!

Nnedimma was very happy. She was particularly happy because she had always craved for a baby girl. The arrival of Ijeabalum had fulfilled that expectation. A girl that would look after her in old age. She sang and thanked God for the 'miracle' as she also called it. She beamed at every visitor with a heartwarming smile. People trooped into the hospital with all kinds of gifts for the child. On the third day, they were discharged from the health centre. They returned to the place they called home.

People continued coming with gifts for the new baby. The baby was wrapped in a soft woolen cloth and laid on a folded mat with some other clothes laid beneath to further soften the hard feel of the mat. Some of the visitors came to partake in the tradition of celebrating the arrival of a new baby which is marked by the rubbing of the native chalk, *nzu* or the baby's powder on their wrist, and then mouth their welcome and congratulations to mother and baby and leave without giving anything.

Some of the visitors pledged to return on a later date to monitor the progress of the newly born baby and the mother. That was the case of a man, an immigrant from another town who lived in the neighbourhood. He was a carpenter. He left and returned with a short stool and a table. He presented them to Nnedimma saying, "Use this table to keep the baby's things, and then keep her on the stool while dressing her up. This baby is a queen and should be treated as such." It sounded prescient. Everybody who heard laughed and that was taken as one of the many pleasantries that could be pronounced to a new baby. But the man persisted, he stood there admiring the baby with so much interest as if they were communicating. He praised her for her beautifully placed long and pointed nose, her beautiful but still half-shut eyes, and her lovely curly hair. He smiled again at the baby and repeated what he had said before. "This is a queen you have here. Do well to treat her as one." He shook the baby's powder into his palms, and lavishly dabbed his neck and face with it and bade them a good evening and left.

✻   ✻   ✻   ✻   ✻

Nneka would smile each time she looked at her baby and recalled what the man had said. She would mutter, "My princess, my queen," as she adjusted the baby's dress and wrapped her well. She wondered what those words really meant and why the man said those words. *Could there be any special meaning to that? Could the baby be royal? Was the father royal? Was Chris from a royal home? Could he be a prince?* But as soon as the thoughts crept up, she quickly discarded them, rationalising why she ought not to entertain them at all. *Why was she even entertaining such thoughts? Does it matter where he came from? What he did to her was abominable and as such should not be mixed up with any fantasy.* She felt bad immediately raising her brows which contorted her face. With that expression, what escaped her mouth was, "Nonsense! What do I care? He has done his worst causing me to drop out of school. I am now a mother instead of a student. I have a baby which no man lays claims to."

Tears dropped from her eyes into her baby's right palm. She wiped it and managed a flicker of a smile amidst the tears that flowed down her cheeks. "I am so happy now that I have you, Ijem. I won't cry again," she said, talking to her baby. Meanwhile the baby stared at her as if she understood what her mother was saying.

⚬‖ *Seven* ‖⚬

Months passed, and just about the time when Ijem turned ten months. One evening, two men sauntered into their compound requesting to see Nneka's mother and her brother-in-law, Patty. When they had been ushered into the hut and all were seated, Nnedimma went into the room and brought kola nuts accompanied with a small kitchen knife and handed them over to Uncle Patty who then presented it to the visitors as was customary saying, "He who brings kola nut, brings life," following up with a native proverb: "O bialu be' onye abia gbuna ya, O naba kwa mkpumkpu apuna ya." With that, he proceeded to break the kola nut. It turned out that the kola nut broke into four pieces. "Ha!" he exclaimed, saying, "this is very good. Four complete market days; *Eke, Orie, Afo, Nkwo,* all have their shares." They all cheered to that.

"That means our mission is approved by our ancestors," Ike chipped in. They ate the kola nut while still exchanging pleasantries and also commenting about the dryness of the weather, given that it was early December. They talked and laughed about the coming Christmas and how the masquerades would add colour and make the whole festive period lively. The fireworks; and how dangerous that could be in dry season as some dry leaves could catch fire, and what that portended for the children who could get hurt and much more. After a few minutes of chattering and some other small talks, there fell a sudden quietness marked by Uncle Patty's body language which indicated it time to get down to the business that brought them.

His posture further signaled to the visitors that it was time for them to shoot. Just then, as if on a cue, Ike, the eldest of the visitors, cleared his throat and came out with what it was that brought them to the house.

"The toad does not run in the afternoon in vain," he began, pausing for what he had just said to sink. Continuing, he added, "It's either the toad is chasing something or something is pursuing it." The others nodded in agreement. He continued, "Without wasting much time, my brother here, Enuma," patting Enuma's shoulder for emphasis (while all eyes turned to look him over for a few seconds), "saw a beautiful apple in your compound and wishes to pluck it." They all laughed for a while.

After the laughter had subsided, Patty cleared his throat and while smiling, asked, "Please, which apple did you people see in this compound and wish to pluck?" Adding quickly, "As you know there are many apples in our household." With the ball played back into their court, Ike and Enuma rose from their seats and stepped aside to put their heads together, while talking in whispers.

Shuffling back into the house with Enuma in tow, both of them took their seats. A second later, Ike stood up, cleared his throat once again and then said, "We are talking about Nneka." Nnedimma smiled, casting a side-long glance at her brother-in-law, Patty inquiringly, and looked down still smiling.

"It's a very good thing you came. Your mission is, indeed, a good one," Patty said. He then turned to Nnedimma and instructed, "My wife, go and fetch our daughter to come and greet our visitors." Nnedimma went in and emerged shortly with Nneka strolling in right behind her.

Nneka wore a loosely fitted gown. The brown gown, with some dash of dull floral patterns sprinkled here and there, did not do justice to her beautiful figure. She walked in abashed and greeted the visitors unenthusiastically. It was quite a surprise they all responded warmly. Taking the cue from their warm reception of her very apparent and coolly delivered greeting, Patty tried to cover up Nneka's very dour entree by smiling a lot more before he delved into introducing the visitors to her; telling her about their mission and finishing up the speech, with, "We'll discuss more later, we just wanted you to greet them." With that, Nneka walked out of their presence with a muted hiss that was only heard by her mother.

Turning his attention back to the visitors, Patty continued, "We have heard what you said. You'll hear from us in a fortnight. Let's talk with our daughter and then, you'll get our response." They concurred. The visitors thanked them and left.

Nneka was angrily pacing about the precinct of the compound when Nnedimma came in after the meeting. Without letting her mother say anything, she lashed out, "Nne, I am not going to marry that man o," Nneka said, pulling at one of her ears. For more emphasis, she continued repeating the same rebuttal over and over again. "I won't marry that man." Adding, "Didn't you see how rough, wretched and irresponsible he looked?" In a barrage, she continued, "I don't like him. So, I won't marry him. I know we are poor but that man's own poverty is screaming! Besides his apparent wretchedness, I'll like to go back to school. My elder sister is not married yet, so why should I be harassed to get married first?"

Nnedimma watched her daughter speak for as long as she wanted. She wanted her to ventilate her frustrations. She could feel her deep sense of disappointment. But deep inside her she wished that Nneka could just accept to marry the man who had mustered the courage to come. All the same she left Nneka to give vent to her misgivings and maybe sleep over the proposal.

A few days later when Nnedimma brought up the discussion,

Nneka flared up, "There is nothing to think about, Nne. I have my answers already. I am not interested. Please, tell them not to bother returning. There is nothing to think about. I won't marry that man for anything, as she proceeded to count off with her fingers, listing his negative qualities. "That man looks ugly, unkempt, hungry…" she reeled off.

"Shut up!" Nnedimma snapped, bidding her daughter to keep quiet. "Don't you ever talk about any man like that again. Don't castigate your potential husband like that."

"He's not my husband! Nne, don't tell me he's my husband!" Nneka snapped, folding her alms beneath her breast while contorting her face in annoyance.

Later in the night when they had retired and lay on their mat, Ihuoma called out in a low tone, "Nneka, N-neka."

Sounding irritated, Nneka asked her sister, Ihuoma, "What's it this time?" Ihuoma raised her head forming a kind of triangle by supporting her head with her palm while her elbow was on the mat. "Do you want to marry that man that came the other day?" Ihuoma asked.

"God forbid!" Nneka hissed.

"I didn't think otherwise myself. That man looked so dirty. Did you look at his face? He couldn't even shave his beards. Yet he was looking for a wife. He could easily be mistaken for Nebuchadnezzar in the Bible," Ihuoma said, throwing her support. Both of them laughed.

Continuing their hushed discussions, Nneka said, "Don't mind Nne and Uncle Patty. I don't even know what they were expecting. Instead of them to just tell them off immediately, they asked them to return in a fortnight."

"But that is the tradition now. Or do you want it to look as if there was a premeditated answer?" Ihuoma asked.

"I don't care whether it would look pre- or post-meditated.

Answer is answer," Nneka scoffed, making a face which Ihuoma did not have the pleasure of seeing because it was dark.

"Anyway, I just don't see a good husband in that man, to say the least," Ihuoma demurred.

"Oh, oh! I didn't know you noticed too," Nneka added. And after the lapse of something when both of them seemed to have run out of what to say, she said, "Please pray, let's sleep." Ihuoma said the prayer and they both laid on their mat each facing opposite directions with their butts stuck out and touching themselves.

✳   ✳   ✳   ✳   ✳

Early in the morning, shortly before the first cock crowed, there was a persistent knock at their door, *kpom, kpom, kpom*. "Nneka and Ihuoma, are you still sleeping?" Nnedimma bawled, followed by another round of knocks. Ihuoma got up, opened the door for her and then stretched her body while she greeted.

"Nne, I hope you slept well, this one you woke up this early?"

"Yes, my dear, I did," Nnedimma said quickly and proceeded to call, "Nneka!"

"Nne," she answered followed up with a groggy, "Good morning."

"Ehn," Nnedimma muttered in return and quickly added, "I want to have a word with you, Nneka."

Nneka sat up, yawned, wiped off sleep from her eyes, and then looked up at her, askance and mumbling, "Nne, I hope all is well this morning?"

"Yes!" she said tersely, waiting for her to fully rouse from her sleep. "Listen, my daughter, I could barely sleep last night. I was full of thoughts about you. I was troubled," she said trailing off from her last word.

"Trouble *kwa*? Troubled about what, Nne?" Nneka asked, searching her mother's face for a clue.

"It was about your suitors. I am afraid you don't seem to be considering Enuma at all for a husband ..." Nnedimma said. Nneka dead panned, keeping mute.

After a few seconds, sensing the confusion her keeping quiet could cause, she spoke, "Nne, you should not worry yourself over that, please! I thought we had settled that issue?"

"No, Nneka, I don't want you to dismiss Enuma just like that yet. I want you to think properly about the whole thing."

"Nne, there is nothing to think about again. If I didn't know you as my mother, I would have been forced to think there was more to this than meets the eye. Why are you goading me on this issue? What is it that you'll gain if I marry that man? He's not even in a position to feed himself not to talk of helping you. Nne! I'm not sure you're seeing properly. I don't know what has come over you. Didn't you see how unkempt and lazy he appeared? *Ehn,* Nne?" she asked. Getting no immediate response from her mother, she said flatly, "No-t-h-in-g," and shrugged her shoulders, with her arms and palms thrown wide apart and open. "Absolutely nothing! So, let me be. And I'd appreciate it so much if we stop talking about this matter. Because there is nothing more to discuss," Nneka snapped.

Nonplussed, Nnedimma continued resting her jaw on her left palm which she'd set up as she watched and listened to her daughter prattle about the inauspiciousness of what she, her mother, was pushing her into. She still remained in that position and was submerged in deep thoughts.

Nnedimma took a deep breath, supporting her frame by placing her left hand on her left knee as she struggled to stand up and leave the room. "Give it more thought, my dear," she trailed off, as she turned and left the room.

Following the tradition for local farmers, it was the season for clearing the land to get it ready for farming as soon as the first rain came. The first rain in the year usually signals the beginning of the planting season. Nneka and Ihuoma were out in the farm and busy clearing their farmland. Their target was to finish the clearing before Christmas.

After about two hours into the work, Nnedimma, who had also accompanied them to the farm, gathered some dry leaves and firewood and started a fire in preparation for roasting some yams for them to eat. They had left the house quite early. Ijem was laid under a shade, on a wrapper that was spread on top of a heap of freshly cut leaves and grasses. "Well-done my warriors. You are women, but then, it's amazing you work like men," Nnedimma said enthusiastically, massaging their egos. "When you get to that mango tree, you should take a break so as to come and eat. By then the yam would be ready," she had added brightly.

"Oh, Nne!" both girls had echoed. The girls worked feverishly, desperately wanting to meet their mother's target quickly so they could go devour the delicacy. A while later, the aroma from the roast yam and *ugba* filled the air adding to the motivation which pushed the girls to double their efforts, but suddenly Ihuoma slacked, and started yawning as if she had not eaten the previous night.

"You are not strong, Ihu. You are so fragile," Nneka teased.

"Says who?" Ihuoma retorted sharply.

"Me, of course," Nneka said and added, "notwithstanding the fact that I'm now *after one*, I am still stronger than you are," Nneka said, rolling her eyes and raising her shoulders.

"You'd wish," Ihuoma replied rather uninterestedly.

Soon after that exchange, Nnedimma, who had overheard them asked them to come and eat, sensing that they had worked hard already. The girls consumed the yam as if they were in competition. "Thanks, Ma," Nneka said while licking up the oil on her fingers. Nnedimma nodded.

"Aha," she exclaimed looking mischievously at Nneka. "My daughter, very soon you'll join your husband and what a blow that would be to me? Ihuoma your sister is not quite as industrious as you. Our farms will suffer," she said.

In protest, Nneka quizzed, "Mama, which husband are you talking about?"

"Enuma! Or do you have another person?" Nnedimma said rather jokingly.

"Please, Mama, don't spoil my day. The sound of that name just sapped my energy. In fact, I'm not working again. I want to go home. I'll come back in the evening or even tomorrow when I regain my strength."

"No! My dear, I didn't mean to upset you. I only confessed my thought," Nnedimma said pleadingly.

"Nne, please keep that thought to yourself," Nneka said matter-of-factly.

"I don't even fancy that Enuma," chipped in Ihuoma.

"Sh!" Nnedimma said with her finger placed across her lips. "What do you know? Your opinion is not solicited on this matter."

"OK!" Ihuoma shouted. Nneka picked up her baby and tied her at the back, with a piece of wrapper, and picked up her hoe and cutlass and headed home. The others followed soon after.

I just wonder why Nne is so interested in this so-called Enuma. She won't even let me breathe, because of Enuma. Everything I do now revolves around Enuma. Hmm, God forbid me marrying that man. Nne had better leave me alone, Nneka thought as she walked home under that afternoon sun.

Later that evening, Nnedimma called Nneka again dwelling on the same issue. "You know I won't deceive you. I cannot push you into fire. Please, I want you to consider getting married to Enuma."

"Why are you pushing me to Enuma? Why, Nne? It's as if you are tired of having me here," Nneka said sharply to her mother.

"No, my child, it's not so." She adjusted her sitting position, moving closer to Nneka as she tried once more to convince her daughter. "See, the truth is: you are not just like every other maiden in this town, the simple reason is because you now have a child."

"E-h, eh! Is that what all these is about? Oh! That's the reason behind all these? I see!" Nneka said wide-eyed as she glared at her mother, as if ready for an open confrontation.

"Yes, my dear," Nnedimma said defiantly. "Listen, your suitors would now be limited. You may not get exactly your choice of a man. And instead of not getting married at all, I'd rather you marry Enuma now that he's still interested." Nneka burst out into tears and slipped into anguish.

"How could Chris do this to me? At least he could have been better than Enuma. Notwithstanding his bestial behaviour, he was educated."

"Don't cry, my dear," Nnedimma offered, trying to pacify her. "This is no time to cry," she said in addition as she wiped Nneka's face with her right palm. "Take it easy, dear," she cooed.

Shaking, Nneka said amidst sobs, "Nne, so what is my fate now? What do I do now?" Not waiting for an answer, she asked her mother rather pointedly, "Won't another man come? Nne, someone who is better than Enuma? Let me wait a while for that man," Nneka pleaded.

"No, my daughter! Time waits for nobody. Maybe before you change your mind, Enuma would already be married to someone else! So, it's a decision you must take now, and within these four walls before they return for our response. Tomorrow is the fortnight. So, what do we tell them when they come if you haven't made up your mind? Remember the adage, 'make hay while the sun shines.'" Nneka kept quite. She kept shaking her head in disbelief.

"I can't believe this. So all my dream of learning French and someday going to Paris would end here in this village? So this is all I will ever live for? Enuma is not educated. I only had my education aborted while in class two. Is this the end of the road in my quest for a better life, for me, and my family? I am being primed up to marry a nonentity just because of what that stupid Chris did to me. God will punish that Chris or whatever his real names are, wherever he is hiding. He is so wicked," Nneka lamented. She squeezed her hands and gnashed her teeth in anguish.

"It's okay," Nnedimma tried to console her.

She sniffed a few times and said stoically, "Since it appears to be the only option that I have ..." she sniffed a few more times. "Do I really have other options?" she asked vaguely. Nne watched her lament in self-pity. At that moment, Nnedimma silently wished she had not talked her into going against her will. *But then what could she have done?* she thought.

"That is the condition we find ourselves. It's well, my daughter. I feel your pain too but I don't want that pain to drag on forever. Once you are married, you face your family life, and you will forget most of these things bugging your mind now," she told her daughter sounding quite unconvincing to her. With that, Nne returned to sleep because it was already 3 o'clock in the morning.

❧‖ *Eight* ‖❧

Enuma and his people came to get their response. They returned in the evening of the next market day to perform a few traditional rites; such as *ime ego,* the paying of the dowry. On that day, Nneka, her mother and other ladies came out in a group to welcome the visitors. During the ceremony, Uncle Patty poured palm wine into a cup and gave it to Nneka. With that cup, it was the tradition for her as a maiden to go in search of her would-be husband and hand it over to him. He, in turn will take the cup and sip some wine out of it signifying that he, indeed, was the right man. Now, with the cup, Nneka went round as if she was searching for the man. Young men leapt forward, jokingly beckoning on her to give them the palm wine. Finally she stopped in front of Enuma, took a sip from the cup and handed the cup over to him. Enuma gulped down the remaining and returned the cup with a token inside, as tradition demanded. At that point, the small crowd jubilated, making merry! Uncle Patty blessed their marriage saying, "Your journey will be likened to that of water, and not that of the firewood." To which everyone present responded by saying: *"I se'*!" "You will beget male and female ..." Uncle Patty continued heaping and pronouncing more blessings, while the crowd responded, *"I se!"*

Two weeks later, Enuma and Nneka wedded in the early morning mass at the Catholic Church in Afanaano. There was no wedding reception or celebration. Enuma could not afford one. And that was the turning point.

✲ ✲ ✲ ✲ ✲

Ijem turned five and started kindergarten. Nneka had another baby girl and became pregnant with the second. She had four more children within eight years marked by poverty, suffering and regret. They all lived in a one-room unfenced apartment. The room served as their bedroom and sitting room. When Nneka had her first baby, it was along the road to the health centre. The second was delivered while she worked in the farm. The third baby, fortunately, got delivered at the health centre. So also was the last and the only boy. To eke out a living, Nneka did all manner of menial jobs. She worked in the farms for others who engaged her for a fee, indulged in various kinds of petty trading just to enable her put food on the table for her children. Her only other help was Ijem.

Enuma, her husband, was entirely a bag of trouble. Even as he was no good at doing anything in helping to provide for the family, he was always at liberty to beat up Nneka at will. He would beat her even when she demanded for money for the basest of the needs in the house. Enuma enjoyed stripping his wife on the road. She would never forget that fateful morning when she was beaten and stripped because she demanded for mere ten naira to buy a bottle of kerosene. He was so bestial that he would not even let her run into the house to get something to cover her nakedness.

If there was anything consistent in their marriage, it was the usual beatings. If he was not beating her, it was Ijem. And if she dared try to stop him, hers will follow. Both mother and daughter had scars on every part of their bodies to show how brutal and abusive Enuma had become. Ijem would cry, and even try hitting the man with anything she could find. In the process, the man would descend on the poor little girl and also beat her up like her mother. The rest of the children who were quite very young would cry as they ran around for help. Sometimes, they would run to Onyeka's house, a neighbour, to call him to come and rescue their mother. Sometimes before he would understand what the little children were mumbling amidst tears, Nneka would have been badly hurt.

When she found the strength, she would visit a chemist for a patch up. She perpetually cried every day in regret. In soliloquy she would gripe: *I never wanted to marry this beast but my mother pushed me and insisted it was the best thing to do. Wouldn't it have been better I stayed unmarried or exercised patience? Maybe by now, I'd have gotten married to a better man. To a man who understands the value of a wife.* Sometimes when she went to the market, and when she interacted with her mates who were lucky in their marriages, her pain became more pronounced. And that normally led her to push the whole blame on her mother who was hell bent on her marrying the *beast* as she had begun to call him.

Visiting the market this particular day, a market day, where her mother traded on stuff, Nneka was overwhelmed by emotions seeing one of her friends whose marriage was good. Racked by bitterness as she sat on an *okpoga* at her mother's stall she burst into tears complaining bitterly. "Nne, wouldn't it have been better if I had stayed unmarried than being in this hell on earth called marriage?" In a barrage, she continued, "Nne, do you know that Enuma smokes marijuana?" Nneka said, wiping the tears that were streaking down her cheeks.

"You don't say!" screamed Nnedimma in shock.

"I am serious, Nne. I saw them when I was looking for a pin in his cupboard. Nne, that is the reason he has no problem or shame in beating me up anyhow. After smoking it, he comes back and treats me as if I'm a football. Nne, I am living in hell with this man you asked me to marry. Nne, I wish I never got into this mess. If that *bastard* who called himself Chris never messed me up, how would I have been seen anywhere near

Enuma?" she cried in grief.

"Take it easy, my dear," Nnedimma said.

"There's nothing to take easy, Nne. I can't take it easy anymore. It's too much for me. It's just too much!" Nneka lamented.

❧| *Nine* |❧

The situation in Enuma's household was always very bleak. As was normal he could barely provide the basic needs of his family; the children were always asked out of school for non-payment of their school fees and other sundry demands. That was exactly the case when Ijem, his step-daughter requested for fifteen naira to pay her school fees. As was usual, Enuma defaulted. Ijem ran to her mother crying. "Ijem, please cry no more. Your tears always break my heart. Wipe your tears, my dear. It will be alright," Nneka said as she comforted her daughter.

"But, Mama, when will it be alright? You always tell me it will be alright."

"Yes, my dear, it sure will," Nneka said tersely.

"Mama, please stop. I need to pay for my report card, and the headmaster said we should not come to school without the money. What do I do? Go to school without the money? Or stay at home? Tell me, Mama, what do I do?" she asked sobbing.

"Hmm!" Nneka heaved, staring at the thatch-roofed ceiling of their kitchen with misty eyes and a heart laden with sorrow. "Don't you worry, my dear. I'll accompany you to the school in order to talk to your headmaster to allow you stay. It shall be well. I'll see what I can do. Now go and prepare for school," Nneka instructed. Ijem made to move but was instantly drawn back by her mother. Staring quizzically at her as she held her firmly, Ijem asked.

"What, Mama?"

Nneka released her grasp and cupped her daughter's tender

and beautiful face between her palms, looking into her eyes and muttering, "I just want you to try to be happy. I love seeing you happy. It makes my heart glow and gives me hope ... *I nu go nwa m?*" she urged. Ijem nodded solemnly, saying nothing. With that she ran into the store to get her navy blue pinafore and white inner shirt from the clothes lines. Her school uniform was already worn out; the formerly white shirt was torn under the left armpit, with ink stains leaving irregular patterns here and there, and with three out of the five buttons of her shirt missing. The navy blue pinafore was no better, there were at least three patches on it.

Ijem retrieved the dresses, slapped them over her right shoulder and held the pile in place with her cheek while she quickly grabbed an empty handless brass bucket with which she scooped a half bucketful of water and rushed to have her bath.

"Mama, I am ready. Are you set?" Ijem shouted enthusiastically.

"Yes, my dear, let's go," Nneka replied, dragging close the only door to their room. The door had unhinged, and had lost its swivel. No thanks to the termites that had dealt with the door frame. She half lifted the door to bring it up to the level of the latch and the hook. She locked the door with an old padlock, and both hurried off to the Afandida Community Central School.

"Good morning, Sir," Nneka greeted the headmaster.

"Good morning, Madam! Please, sit down," Mr Onyeizu said waving her to have a seat.

"Thank you, Sir," Nneka said making herself comfortable.

Looking up from across his desk, he asked, "How may I help you?"

Nneka leaned forward to bridge the gap and said, "I am Mrs Enuma," as she adjusted once again to say, "Ijem Obidi's mother."

"Yes, Madam, I hope all is well, Madam?"

"Yes," she said quickly, adding, "all is well, Headmaster. But I came to ask you for a small favour. Could you please allow my daughter into the class today? She has told us about the money for her report card." Not wasting any time, she quickly offered, "I will try to raise the money before the end of today," she said pleadingly.

"Madam, asking the pupils to pay before being allowed into their classes is the only way we get most of them to pay up. You are well aware that the school term will soon end, and that means we would need to prepare their report cards. You know it's not the obligation of the teacher to pay ... I cannot pay for her, Madam," the headmaster said.

"I know, Sir. I know. But all I'm asking is that you just give me today. By tomorrow she must come with the money," Nneka assured the headmaster.

After a little while, Mr Onyeizu said, "Okay, Madam, just today."

"Thank you," Nneka said profusely as she rose from her seat.

Ijem ran out from where she had been hiding beside the headmaster's window and hugged her mother when she stepped out of the headmaster's office.

"Thank you very much," she said happily.

"It's okay. Now run to your class. You are late," Nneka told Ijem. She watched her daughter disappear into her class.

In a bid to keep her promise, Nneka went home immediately. She took a machete, a basket and a hoe and went to the farm in search of remnants of cassava tubers since the new ones were yet to mature for harvesting. She was able to gather a sizeable quantity which she hauled back home. Her intention was to sell the cassava in the early morning market of the next day before the school's resumption time. That was not to be. Enuma stormed into the house from one of his usual outings drunk. Nneka sensing his mood, served him *akpu* and *ofe onugbu*. Although he did not provide for the food, he inspected the food for large chunks of meat but was disappointed when he saw only pieces of dry fish. This set him off. He charged to the backyard where Nneka was busy arranging the cassava she had harvested in a basket. He angrily demanded where she got the cassava from and for what purpose. She had scarcely provided the answer before Enuma grabbed the machete and started chopping the cassava tubers into useless sizes. Nneka tried to stop him. That earned her hot slaps which left her dazed for a while.

⟨⊘‖ *Ten* ‖⊘⟩

"Each time you return home, you have food to eat," Nneka thundered. She was in a very foul mood. She was upset and frustrated about her husband's unyielding attitude. "You have never bothered asking where the money comes from. The drugs I bought for our son two days ago is finished. I didn't ask you for money to buy those. Yet you complain about the absence of big chunks of meat in your soup? You don't even care to know how your children are faring," she said tailing off, and eyeing him in a condescending manner and then completing the routine with a huge derogatory smirk. Enuma who had not uttered a word since she began to speak, laughed. The little laugh he let out, a guffaw was always a prelude to him getting violent, and Nneka this time around was unafraid and couldn't care less!

"I should not eat?" Enuma asked menacingly. "Now, I know you want to starve me to death. Bad woman!" Enuma said harshly.

"Please, just give me the money," Nneka said, standing her ground and adding, "I am not ready for your troubles this morning. Just give me the money to buy the drug for our son. He's shaking there on the mat with fever and all you can offer is talk about whether you are entitled to eat or not," she said with an outstretched hand insisting that he gives her the money.

"Come and dip hands into my pocket and get the money. I can see that you have grown wings," he said fiercely.

Irritated by her continuous nagging, he sprang up on his feet and turned to leave the house. Nneka followed on his heels. He spun quickly and lashed out, whacking her face with rapid and unexpected slaps. She bent down and seized one of his legs, sinking her teeth into his laps, resolving to be killed instead of letting him get away with beating her up without her doing something. She was no match but she held her grounds, biting and scratching his entire legs, and whatever part of the body she could get hold of. At the end of the scuffle, Enuma beat up his wife black and blue, redesigning her face as usual.

The next day she hobbled off to the market to meet Nnedimma. "Nne, this man will kill me one day. I get beaten up for every little thing I say. And for every little demand, even for the health of our children. Nne, for how long will this continue? How long, Nne?" she asked, as tears streamed down her swollen and battered cheeks. As usual, Nnedimma remained taciturn but a closer look at her would reveal that she was deeply upset, and lost in deep thoughts ... In her agony, she drew her daughter close, and comforted her.

When Nnedimma got home she spoke to her two sons, Emeka and Chiazo. "Enuma will kill your sister if care is not taken."

"*Aru*! That's an abomination!" screamed Emeka.

Nnedimma continued, grim-faced. "This man beats your sister at will. He's a good-for-nothing husband, yet he derives maximum pleasure in *panel-beating* my daughter. Each time you see Nneka, she looks so pale, horrible and tattered. Regardless of what he's done to her she still manages to remain his wife; cooking and serving him food according to what she is able to whip up. But that does not satisfy him. Instead he expects a king's portion while he never bothers to give her money to cook. This is too much. I will appreciate it if both of you can go and talk sense into that man's head." Her two sons who had listened without saying a word nodded in unison.

But then after a little while one of them broke the silence. "Nne, please be strong. It's unfortunate this is happening. We shall surely pay him a visit tomorrow morning. We shall pay him a visit and let him know that Nneka has brothers who can fight for her," Emeka said solemnly.

"No! Emeka," Nnedimma interrupted him promptly. "I am not sending you to go and fight Enuma. I just want you to go and talk to him. Talk to him as men. Talk to him to stop beating my daughter," she said while raising both hands to signify that she meant just that, and nothing more.

"Nne, leave this matter to us, we will handle it when we get there. We are not going there to fight but if that man refuses to learn his lesson, we will teach him in the language we know he understands better."

"He has bitten more than he can chew this time," Chiazo said narrowing his already reddened eyes. Emeka and I will storm his house first thing tomorrow morning," he added.

"No! I think I should come with you," Nnedimma said sensing that if she didn't accompany them to Enuma's house the situation may degenerate into a bloody fisticuffs.

"No. Nne, you need not follow us. We will go there with our motorcycle and that can only take both of us. Don't worry. It will go well. Okay?" Emeka said patting his mother's shoulders reassuringly.

It was early Saturday morning, and Nneka was busy packing the dirt she swept out from the kitchen and the ashes from the previous day's cooking when her brothers rode into the open compound. "Brother, brother, brother," she heard her children calling out as they ran out to welcome their uncles. Nneka quickly washed her hands and wiped them on her wrapper. She came out to welcome her brothers. "*Nno nu o!*" she greeted. Barely returning her greeting, both of them walked up close to her to look at her face. Their countenances changed. Their tone changed immediately.

"Sister, where is Enuma?" Chiazo asked. "Where is that ingrate you call a husband? Did you say he's the one that did this to you? Oh my God! That beast did this to you?" the fuming Chiazo prattled. Nneka nodded repeatedly and could not utter a word as she had already been overwhelmed by emotions. Tears rolled down her cheeks.

All this while Emeka kept quiet, watching with eyes that had already narrowed. Speaking through clenched teeth, Nneka said, "Please, come in and sit down, he will soon be back from work. You know he does security job at Ochi health centre."

They all went into the room and sat down. The children started feasting on the *akara* that their uncles had bought on their way. At the top right corner of the room stood a very old black and white television which Enuma used when he was living in Benin as a bachelor. The television had never worked since it was brought into the house because they had no electricity. At the left corner of the room, close to the wall, were bags containing the children's clothes and their mother's. The only window and door were on the same side of the room. The single roomed house was roofed with a couple of old rusted zinc. There was no ceiling. The floor was partially covered with an old torn red carpet.

Soon enough as Nneka had stated, Enuma stepped in. "Good morning, in-law," Emeka and Chiazo chorused in veiled affectation disguising their anger.

"Good morning," Enuma replied enthusiastically. He dropped his baton beside his chair and sat down.

He offered them kola nut as was the tradition but Emeka declined the offer saying, "Please, let's forget the kola for now and discuss what has brought us this morning."

Enuma, shrugged, and then grimaced as he asked, "I hope all is well? What could be so urgent or important that will make you reject an early morning kola? Hmm. Okay then …" he said as he sat back in his old couch, expectantly, with his two hands tightly gripping the arm rest of the couch.

"Enuma," Emeka called out as he started. "My brother and I came this morning with the single purpose to ask you a few questions. The questions are in respect of Nneka. One, did we commit a crime by giving you our sister in marriage? What are you doing to Nneka, our sister? Our sister is supposed to be looking her best, as a married woman. Instead each time we see her, she would be bearing one mark or the other which she sustained from your frequent beatings. Look at her face. Just look at how puffed her face looks because she demanded money from you to buy your son's drug!"

"Eh, eh," Enuma said interrupting him and disagreeing with him.

"Allow me to finish, Enuma," snapped Emeka in anger. Chiazo was already shaking his two legs visibly irritated at his elder brother and their brother-in-law's exchange of words. *I am not in the mood to waste words on this beast,* Chiazo thought as he got up and started to pace about, and then he suddenly stood still to fix a stern gaze at Enuma.

"Enuma, we did not come here this morning to entertain these stories. We have just come to warn you to please stop beating our sister. If you do not value her, please, we do value her so much. If you are looking for where to flex your muscles, I suggest that you sign up and enter the boxing or wrestling ring. Stop *panel-beating* my sister, Enuma. I may not be this patient the next time this happens," Emeka warned.

"Get out!" Enuma shouted, standing up. "I said get out from my house. Who are you? Who are you to come to my house to talk rubbish? You came here this early morning to defend this thing you call sister?" Enuma said, pointing his left hand at Nneka, who was already uncomfortable at the turn the discussion was taking.

Enuma continued, "Look at who is talking. You good-for-nothing fool. You are telling me to go to the ring ... What meaningful thing have you been doing with your own life to advise someone? If men are talking, you too will talk. What can you boast of? Your mother's mud house is falling apart, and you are here to warn me," he said with a lot of sarcasm dripping from his mouth.

Emeka who had been trying so hard to hold down his temper as Enuma ranted, looked straight into Enuma's eyes and asked him, "Are you talking to me like that? It's not enough that you've been maltreating our sister. You have the effrontery to talk to me in that manner?"

"Emeka! Shut your mouth. What do you know? Have you asked your sister how she has been misbehaving? If she continues to misbehave, I'll beat her until she learns how to respect a man. And there's nothing you both or ten of you put together can do to stop me," Enuma boasted.

"Enuma, you are asking for trouble and daring us by asking what we will do about you beating up our sister," Emeka said, inching his way towards Enuma. "Enuma, are you still asking? You really want to know what I can do, eh?" Emeka asked as he looked Enuma square in the face with eyes almost tightly closed. "Enuma, do not, I repeat, do not dare me," Emeka thundered.

Just then, Enuma rushed and picked up his baton and attempted hitting Emeka on the head. "If you don't leave my house this minute, they will take away your corpses here," Enuma threatened. Emeka seized his hand in the air and snatched the baton from him. A fight ensued. Both of them dragged him outside the room and gave him the beating of his life.

Nneka ran helter-skelter, trying to stop them. She cried as she called on them to stop. "You will kill him. Please, stop." Enuma lay sprawled in a heap, crying. They took Nneka and her children away even as he lay down there, snivelling.

✧‖ *Eleven* ‖✧

As Ijem turned ten she had no expectation of celebrating her birthday. She had never experienced it except when she turned nine which coincided with the award giving day of the school. It was going to be another long holiday for her. Her mother knowing she had not had any experience of a birthday, took her to attend a birthday party of their neighbour's five-year-old son. There, Ijem, ate cake for the first time, and had a bottle of soft drink alone. That was an experience she would never forget in a hurry.

As she turned ten she entered primary six. She was looking forward to being in the most senior class of the primary school. She thought, *who would be the school captain in our class? Maybe Elochukwu. Yes, it should be him because he is tall and huge. The junior pupils will be afraid of him making them to obey him during the period for manual labour. Or would they appoint Ugo? No, Ugo is very intelligent but too quiet to cope with the pupils in our school. He is also not strong. The big boys in the class could beat him up.* She smiled at her imaginations. All these thoughts and the promise that her mother had made to make her, at least, a new white inner shirt kept her imagining what it would feel like on the first day in primary six. She painted a picture of herself in a new white uniform. She was really basking in the euphoria of the new school uniform because all she had ever worn to school were given to her by their neighbour's children who either changed a new one or those she inherited from the ones that had graduated from primary school and going to college. These thoughts and imagination kept Ijem very happy and excited.

✡ ✡ ✡ ✡ ✡

"Ijem!" thundered her step-father from the room.

"Sir!" she answered as she ran towards him.

"Come here, what have you been doing since morning? And what time is it?" he asked.

"I have been sweeping the whole compound and now I am packing the waste," she said with a shaky voice out of fear. Without warning, he slapped her.

"So, since morning, you have been sweeping the compound? How big is the compound? Go and buy me snuff. Stupid girl! You are too lazy for all the food you consume in this house. I don't know why I should be wasting my money on a bastard whose father is unknown. Nonsense!" he said as he waved her away from his presence. Sobbing, she collected the snuff box and some money as she dashed out of the room. He spat on the ground, and told her to make sure she returned before it dried up. She sobbed and ran through the errand. Coming back quickly, she made to hand over the little box to him. "Keep it on that table." She dropped it quickly and turned to leave the room. "Come here." She turned sharply, trembling with fear. "Go and get the flask, and put food in the feeding bottle for my son." She rushed to the corner where the flask was kept. Just at the door, she missed her step, hit the door and fell down. The flask fell off her hands and shattered. Her toe started bleeding as it had scraped the rough edge of the door frame. Enuma jumped up immediately reaching out for his cane, and started whipping the poor girl mercilessly. Even while she was sprawled on the floor. She screamed as the cane landed randomly on her buttocks, back, thighs, and calves. She rolled away and dashed out into the compound running like a mad girl while running her hands all over her body. He started chasing after her. In a bid to reach her he threw the broom that he had just taken. It landed on her forehead and she fell down. She stopped sobbing and lay down there on the ground, lifeless. Just then, her mother entered the compound with a basket on her head. Seeing her daughter on the floor, she quickened her steps.

"What is going on, Enuma? What happened to Ijem?" she queried as she dumped the basket that she was carrying at the centre of the compound. She rushed over to where her daughter lay. She lifted her, calling out, "Ijem, Ijem, Enuma, what happened to my child?" Seeing blood on her forehead, she shouted on top her voice, "Enuma *egbuo mo*! Hey! Ijem." She reached for a bucket of water as she called on her neighbours. In a jiffy, the compound was filled with people. She poured half of the water on her and started dabbing her body with the rest. Mrs Agina, a neighbour, fanned the girl at the same time. After a while, Nneka lifted Ijem with the help of Mrs Agina. Tying her on her back, she started running and crying to the hospital. Onyeka who was just returning home from the market with his wife offered to rush the little girl to the hospital. Before evening, Ijem opened her eyes in the hospital. She had a serious headache, and a swollen face. Her whole body ached as she cried. Her mother wept too. Just then, her grandmother, Nnedimma, came into the hospital with edible things she had bought from the market. She had been informed of what happened by her daughter's neighbours.

"I am taking this child before Enuma kills her for me. I am taking her. I don't have a little girl to stay with yet," Nnedimma declared. "That man's heart is behind. He is so wicked. He beats both child and mother, he is so heartless. I won't let him kill this girl. Not in my life. No ..." she said determined to carry out her intention. "I let Ijem stay with you people till now because you also needed help. But heaven would blame me if anything happens to this little girl. *Tufiakwa*! *Nwa m*, she said as she rubbed Ijem's hands and blew air over her swollen face. Sorry, *nwa m*, *ndo nne m*, I am here now, nobody will touch you again."

"Mama *nnukwu*," Ijem murmured.

"Ijem," she responded.

"My head aches badly, and my body hurts."

"*Ndo, nwa m*," Nnedimma said with her face depicting exactly how bad she felt for the pains her grandchild was going through. "I will take you home with me," she reassured her again.

"Enuma!" Idigo called shaking her head in disbelief. "How can a man hate a little child so much? How can someone beat a child as if he was fighting his mates. Hmm," she shrugged her shoulders. The three of them ate the food that she had brought. They spent the night in the hospital.

Early the next morning, Mr Isaac who was a family member of the Okwueze family came and settled the hospital bill, and paid for the drugs. He drove them home. Enuma was snuffing while sitting on the edge of his old stretcher when they arrived. He got up and blew his nose to get rid of some dark brown remnants of the stuff he had just ingested. Mr Isaac went straight to Enuma and said, "I have warned you severally to look for your fellow men each time you want to show your strength, and stop killing your wife and children. I have never raised a finger on my wife for over twenty years. It is not because she does not get me angry or because she is a saint, or anything like that. Rather, it is my decision. To me, a man should never beat his wife and children. I'd rather talk to them. If you must beat your children, then do that only mildly remembering they are just children. Their bones are still too tender to withstand your manly force. Beware, Enuma, else you would kill somebody, someday. I am going."

He consoled the little girl, and gave Nnedimma two hundred naira. He patted Nneka's back saying, "Please, take it easy, Nne." He turned and walked to his car as they watched. Nneka wished she could switch husbands. Ijem followed him, crying.

"I want to go with you, uncle. He would beat me again." He

squatted in front of the girl. Holding her cheeks, he wiped her tears, and promised to always check on her. "He won't beat you again. Don't worry, my dear." He took her to Nnedimma, "Stay with Mama." She nodded in agreement still looking up at him as he walked back to his Peugeot 505 ash-coloured car. Tears filled her eyes. Ijem held her grandmother and cried the more. Nnedimma looked at the little girl with so much pity.

"Nneka, please let me have her things. I am taking her home now." They gathered Ijem's things and she finally left her step-father's house to live with her grandmother.

✵   ✵   ✵   ✵   ✵

"Mama *nnukwu*," Ijem called after eating yam and *ugba* which was her favourite at her grandmother's place.

"My dear, what is it? Feel free to tell me anything," she added. "This is your home. This is where you belong. Nobody will maltreat you here. *I nu go*?"

"Mama, I will get back at him when I grow up. I will arrest him with police. I will not let any man beat me up like that again when I grow. Mama, couldn't you have brought my mother too? That man will always beat her now that I am no longer there and there would be nobody to help her. I hate what that man does. He takes pleasure in beating me and my mother. I don't want him to beat my mother again. Mama Nnukwu, please, let's go and get my mother, please. Let's bring all of them here. Please, Mama," Ijem pleaded.

"Your mother is married to Enuma and so I don't have the right to take her away from her husband's house."

"Mama, even if the man kills her?" she asked, with her inquisitive eyes wide open.

"He won't do a thing like that."

Mama *nnukwu*, it's because you have not witnessed that man beating my mother," she said and burst out again in tears.

"Nothing will happen to Nneka. God will not let anything

happen to her."

"Mama, have you seen all the scars on my mother's face?" Ijem asked, looking up at Nnedimma as she nodded. "They were inflicted by him. No man will do that to me when I grow up. I will deal with that man. I will find a way and deal with him."

"No one will dare do that to you, dear. Not in my life," Nnedimma swore. She reached out again, massaging Ijem's wound with *okwuma*, after washing the wound with the local soap. Later they retired to their hut and slept. Ijem worried about her mother and step-siblings. "Who knows if they had anything to eat this night," she thought. Ijem cried and drifted off to sleep. In her sleep, she had a dream where a large crowd gathered in her honour; television stations covered the event, and many people cheered her. She was overwhelmed. She saw many great things happening; she was in the company of many great people. She was addressing the crowd when Nnedimma called at her to get up for morning prayers. She was disappointed to see that they were still in the old mud house.

"Mama, why did you bring me back? Why, Mama?"

"Bring you back from where?" inquired Nnedimma. Ijem jumped up from her mat, yawning.

"Mama you were eating chicken and wine ... how come you have finished eating your food so fast?" Nnedimma laughed and stared at Ijem in confusion. "What is funny, Nne?"

"It's you, my child. The last chicken I ate was when you were born when we slaughtered a big fowl in celebration. So, I don't see how you just saw me eating chicken and drinking some foreign wine instead of my usual palm wine." She laughed again. "I have never tasted foreign wine before. I only wonder what it tastes like."

"What are you saying? Never tasted wine before? At your age, Nne? Hmm, it's unbelievable," she said. "But don't worry. I will buy you cartons of wine when I grow up. Different types ..." she promised with smiles.

"I know you will do that, my dear." Nnedimma hugged her granddaughter. Few minutes later, Ijem sat down thinking about her dream before they knelt down to pray. Nnedimma prayed, and also committed Ijem's dream to God for its fulfilment.

✂| Twelve |✂

It was three days to the resumption date of the new school year. Ijem grew quite apprehensive, and uncertain about her school plans. She was filled with all kinds of negative thoughts about her education: *will Nne let me continue at my former school? Or is she going to enrol me in another school? No, the new school may draw me back. They may offer me a lower class. I'll really want to continue where I stopped ...* Recalling the upcoming event of selecting a new school captain she wondered what the outcome would be. *Hmm, who knows. Who will be the school prefect among those boys? I would really want to witness it. God, please let me go back to my school. But the distance from here is much. How can I make it to school from here every day? God! This is another huge task if I must continue at my school.* She rested her lean frame quietly on the old shaky bench at the pavement. *Which is a better option for me now? Dropping a class in a closer school or walking the far distance daily to my school? Hmm ...* She paced about the compound she had meticulously swept with long brooms earlier. She stopped near the goat's stead, watched the goats eat the palm fronds she had harvested from the little palm trees in their farm. *But I can make it to my school if I wake up very early.* She imagined the distance. *Ah! But that will really be strenuous for me doing the to and fro daily. Well, that may be my price for at least having rest of mind which I didn't have at my step-father's house. I can give anything to avert his constant scolding, beatings and molestation.* She continued pacing about the compound till she got out of the shade and went out into the sun. She paused to observe the position of her shadow. *Oh, it's lunch time. Nne will soon return from the market.* She walked briskly into the house and brought out some *ji anunu*. Picking up a charcoal and grease-laden pot, she began preparing lunch. She was about starting the fire with dry leaves and firewood when Nnedimma came in carrying a bunch of leaves most of which were still on their stems. The consignment was for her oil bean business. She lowered the bunch. "Welcome!" Ijem greeted her grandmother enthusiastically.

"Hmm, *nwam*, what are you doing?"

"I want to boil yam," Ijem said in an upbeat manner adding, "so we can eat it with palm oil."

"Okay, that's good but we shall add *anyu* to it so that they will serve as dinner for us," Nnedimma said as she took a knife and went to the garden in front of the compound and returned shortly, carrying a bunch of *ugboguru* leaves and a ball of *anyu*. She quickly cut the *anyu* into four pieces, arranged them in the pot adding the yams on top. "Ijem, over to you now," she said walking out of the kitchen.

Ijem took the pot and its content and placed it on top of the fire that she had set. Nnedimma came into the kitchen minutes later to add the *ugboguru* into the boiling pot. Soon, it was done. Nnedimma drained off the water by tilting the pot with one end of it pointing downward while the cover was slightly shifted to allow the water to run off. She removed the *ugboguru* that had been made tender and put it in a wooden mortar for Ijem to pound. She peeled one of the yams and added it into the mortar. The yam was to serve as a thickener for the local sauce. When it was well mixed, Nnedimma added some red palm oil that she had melted by keeping the bottle near the fire while Ijem turned the pestle to achieve a smooth blend. She added salt to taste, and the food was ready. While they ate, they discussed Ijem's school and finally agreed that she will continue at her former school where she would finish her primary six.

On Monday morning, Ijem arrived school early despite the long distance she had walked. She arrived in her immaculate white uniform which her mother had bought for her. Nneka had sent the dress across to her on Sunday evening. She looked quite radiant and clean in the new uniform. Her grandmother, on her own part, had skilfully scraped her hair with a sharp razor blade on Saturday. With that clean shave, she looked quite set for the new school year.

In school, the pupils were all milling around, exchanging pleasantries and happy to see their friends. The major gossip that was trending centred on the likely naming of a new school prefect that very day. In fact, there were speculations in respect of who was going to be the school prefect. The pupils chattered noisily in the class before the assembly time. They speculated that the new captain would be announced during the morning assembly. "It will certainly be Ugo," Nneoma said.

"Liar!" screamed Adaora. "It will be Eloo!"

"Hmm, says who?" queried Chika in response to Adaora's suggestion. "I have strong feelings it will be Nnanna. Nnanna is not only tall, he's also fairly intelligent," Chika said.

"Well," Ijem interrupted, "I think it will be Ugo. Forget the height, Ugo is very intelligent. Eloo only has height. He does not know anything. He is a dullard and a bully champ," she said, looking furtively on both sides to ensure no one else heard her. She knew the implication of Eloo getting to hear that she called him names.

"But if not for the fact that you are a small girl, I would have said you will make a good captain," Adaora teased Ijem.

Ijem made a face, rolling her eyes and said, "Me? Who dash monkey?" Just at that moment the assembly bell sounded in its characteristic manner.

The girls ran off to the assembly ground with all of them struggling to stand closest to the front line. They went through the normal assembly routine of songs and prayers. They all sang with high spirits, given their expectations. After the announcements, nothing was said of the school captain. The pupils went back to their classes disappointed.

After the first lesson, the headmaster sent for the primary six teacher, popularly called Aunty Uche. She was an elegant, intelligent, round faced, young woman in her late twenties. Soon, she and the headmaster stood in front of the primary six pupils talking in low tones and looking at the pupils. The atmosphere was tense as the pupils did not exactly know what the small talk between them was all about.

Nnanna, the class captain, hit the desk four times with his right palm: *gbam, gbam, gbam, gbam*. The pupils all stood up and greeted the headmaster in their normal chorale manner, "Gooood morning, Sir!"

"Good morning, class ... sit down," came his own immediate response. Without wasting time, the headmaster said, "If you hear your name, step out. Nnanna Obi, Elochukwu Ike, Ugochukwu Aja, Chika Onoh and Ijem Obidi." The pupils filed out with mixed feelings. As they stood, they began to whisper among themselves, "What did we do, Ijem?" Chika asked, trembling in fear.

"How would I know?" replied a confused Ijem.

"Follow me," said the headmaster as he walked back to his office with Aunty Uche in tow. After talking with each of the pupils separately, he sent them back to the class.

Returning to the class, the rest of the class asked them why they were so called, but they could not make out anything intelligible from their responses. The second lesson started. Soon, they went for short break and returned to their classes. No sooner had they settled down expecting to commence the next lesson than the headmaster asked the pupils to reconvene at the assembly ground.

"As you all know," he began, "it is a new school year and as is the tradition, it's time for us to choose a new school captain." The mood of the assembly changed. The pupils started murmuring; the murmur sounded like a buzzing sound as they talked to one another. "Keep quiet!" the headmaster yelled. "Quiet!" he yelled yet again. Calm returned immediately to the assembly. "The post of the school captain is a very important one, and it is our tradition to consider all criteria before choosing who will occupy that position for each academic year. After due consultations with the teachers ..." he paused, "a substantive school captain has emerged, and would be announced to you shortly." He turned again to talk with the teachers. The tension was now palpable. There was a pin-drop silence. The pupils waited with bated breath. Their eyes darted in all directions; sometimes settling in the direction of Eloo, who stood with so much confidence. The headmaster cleared his throat once again. He did not immediately speak, enjoying the atmosphere he had engendered by pushing the pupils to keep speculating in their minds as they stood waiting. Finally he said; "May I have the pleasure of announcing to you ..." he took a moment again to survey the assembly. "The new school captain of Afandida Community Central School for the current academic year is no other person than ... Ijem Obidi!"

"Hey!" came a thunderous scream from the pupils, expressing great surprise. Ijem stood transfixed, mouth agape as she started sobbing quietly. Adaora shouted, "I said it, I told you, I knew it, I saw it coming ... "Congratulations, Ijem!" she said as she rushed to hug the overwhelmed newest school captain. Ijem was speechless.

"Ijem Obidi step out," the headmaster said, smiling. As she stepped forward, there followed a deafening applause ... They continued applauding and chanting some celebratory songs:

"Winner, oh, winner!
Winner, oh, winner!

Ijem you don win oh, winner!
I say you go win forever oh, winner!"

The girls were particularly happy that the school authority had chosen a female as the captain. It was the first time in the history of the school. Some of the boys who had been expectant had their expectations dashed. Elochukwu in particular was crestfallen as he had bragged about being the next school captain. Ijem stood before the entire assembly and could barely move due to the shock she had just experienced. She thought herself to be the least to have been considered for the coveted position of the school captain. Her thoughts raced: *How can I possibly be a school captain with all these big boys and big girls in my class and all the pupils in this school? How am I going to function? No, no, this can't possibly be true.* Amidst her fears, thoughts and the excitement that engulfed her, she managed to flash a coy smile as the pupils hailed her. She was eventually decorated with the captain's cap and badge. The pupils clapped and screamed out of excitement.

"Attention!" the headmaster continued yelling until calm was restored. He spoke, presenting Ijem formally, and admonishing the pupils to respect their new school captain. "Age, height and physical appearance were not part of the criteria used in deciding who the school captain should be," he said. "Ijem possesses all the qualities of a substantive school captain. I do not want to get any report of any pupil insulting, disrespecting, or abusing her due to her young age. In fact, her age should make all of you to accord her greater respect. She is just ten and I know many of you here are older than that. But if you offend her, you have offended the school. You also offend me and you know the implication ..." he said. The headmaster turned to Ijem. "Do you have anything to say?" he asked. All eyes were now trained on her.

The shy little girl just muttered, "I want to say a big thank you to the school authority for having faith in me. I know becoming the school captain demands a lot to be done. I will put in my best to be the best school captain ever." This was greeted by a loud scream and applause.

They all returned to their classrooms and talked about the new school captain for the most part of the day. Before Ijem got home, the news had spread all over the village. She noticed as she walked home that people were staring and pointing in her direction. That was when she started feeling the weight of her new position. She was happy. She smiled intermittently to herself.

But why was I chosen? Why was I the preferred choice? Hmm. God, help me please! she mused. She unlatched the wooden gate and ran down the slopy entrance to the house. "Nne!" she yelled several times as she ran into the house. Nnedimma answered from the kitchen.

"Nwam, are you back?"

"Yes, Nne, good afternoon! Nne, I am now the new captain of our school." Nnedimma paused and took a moment off from what she was doing; she was grating cocoyam with a local grater made with a flattened roofing zinc that was perforated with nails and fastened on a wood.

"*Caftin!*" she exclaimed, mispronouncing the word 'captain'. "What does that mean? Do you mean you'll no longer go to school?" asked the very confused woman.

"No, Nne, I am now the head of all the pupils in my school. Nne, see my new badge and my special cap," she prattled, touching both badge and cap.

"Hmm! Eh! Ijem, gi nwa onyisi? You, the head?" she asked pointing at her.

"Yes!" Ijem responded, jumping up excitedly, wearing proud smiles.

"That's very good, my daughter. That is good, my dear. I am happy. I am not surprised because I know you are born to lead."

She hugged her with her left hand because tiny shreds of cocoyam had messed her right hand. And she was aware that cocoyam could be itchy when it got in contact with any part of the body which was exposed to it. "Now go and change into your house clothes, then come and let's prepare this *mbughu*. At least we can celebrate with it," she said happily. Ijem went inside the house, dropped the polythene bag, which served as her school bag and turned up few minutes later in her regular oversized house wear.

❧ Thirteen ❧

It was September, the beginning of a new school year. And Ijem had taken and passed her common entrance examination and was about proceeding to college. "Good morning, pupils!"

"Good morning, Sir," echoed the pupils of Afandida Community Central School. "Stay in line, I don't want to see anyone who is not properly dressed to school. I don't want to see anyone wearing a games' wear because today is Monday, and you are supposed to put on your white and navy blue uniform, is that right?"

"Yes, Sir!" the pupils responded.

Caught off guard, Obi, who was not properly dressed, exclaimed, "What do I do now? Hey, God, I am in trouble!" he kept on saying. Soliloquizing, he told himself, *Obi, you are in trouble. What do I do?* Just then, the headmaster spotted him.

"Hey! You! Come out!" the headmaster ordered. With a very shaky voice and eyes filled with tears Obi came forward, walking uncertainly.

As soon as he approached the headmaster he started pleading, "I am sorry, Sir. It will not happen again. Sir, please!"

"Shut up! What's your name and what class are you in?"

"Basic 5, Sir."

"So, why did you come to school in your games' wear? Don't you have a school uniform?"

"I, I, I..." Obi stammered in tears. He dreaded the cane so much.

"Kneel down, hands up and open your mouth before I lose

my temper," the headmaster commanded.

"Sir, my uniform ... It's torn and my mother said she'll amend it today when she goes to the market. Please, Sir, I will wear it tomorrow. I am sorry," he said profusely as tears flowed freely down his cheeks. The headmaster raised the cane as if to whip him but lowered it on a second thought.

"Now, the rest of you line up properly and listen up. Tell the following people or their parents to come for their first school leaving certificates."

After reeling out several names, he told them that the following candidates made distinctions.

"Ijem Obidi ... and Onyema Iwu."

The list would be posted on the school's noticeboard. Kindly notify them immediately to come for their certificates," he said and left for his office.

"Hmm! Wonders shall never end. Ifii, can you imagine? Ijem's result is different. What does the headmaster mean?" Chinenye asked, looking quite astonished.

"Hmm, me, I wonder too. But my confusion is that she was always coming first or second position throughout her years in this school. She was even made the school captain. All the teachers talked about her. Even our teacher constantly use her as an example in our class. She was always winning prizes. I always admired her. But why is it that her own result is different? I hope she did not fail," said Ifeoma, also looking concerned.

"I hope so too," Chinenye chipped in. "Let's take the road that passes by the church so that we can stop by their house and tell her mother about what the headmaster said," Chinenye suggested.

"Okay," Ifeoma agreed. "I think that is a good idea so they can confirm from the school why she should have a different result. See, even an *iti* like Chike passed along with the others. Maybe we are making a mistake. Is it not possible that it could be the best kind of result like she has always done?"

"I don't know," Ifeoma replied.

"Please, let's stop worrying our small heads over this matter.

Her mother will see to that when she meets with the headmaster," Chinenye stated.

"Okay, if you say so!" Ifeoma said, surrendering. They walked silently, both pondering on the possible explanation to the difference in Ijem's result.

Chinenye broke the silence. "That reminds me, Ifii, please, do you people have spent palm fronds? If you do then I can come and fetch some for tomorrow's handiwork. Please, I wouldn't want to be punished by the headmaster."

"Yes, we have, but I intend to use them for mine," she told her. "But we can share what is available and possibly get more from Mama Ngo's house. They cut many palm fronds last week," Ifeoma added.

"Okay, thank you. I will come in the evening," Chinenye said excitedly. With that they both ran to Enuma's house and delivered the message to Enuma and his wife, Nneka.

Enuma burst out laughing upon receiving the message. He was just obsessed and self-centred. Anything that would diminish his wife and his step-daughter was good. Even when he did not understand the import of what the word 'distinction' meant. He wished it was disaster that it portended. "I knew it! I said it that I was wasting my money on that bastard. I wasted my money, my food, my energy," he went on. "*Mtchew,*" he sneered. "Now she has failed. *Odawaru ukwu*, she has failed woefully. She has proven to the world that she is a good-for-nothing little brat. Let her thank her stars that she is no longer living in my house. If not, I would have skinned her alive," he said, feeling good at the thought that his step-daughter had failed her primary six examination.

"Enuma, what is it again?" Nneka sharply retorted, dropping the corn she was eating? "Why do you detest that little girl so much? All you have exhibited in the past ten years towards her has been pure vitriol. Even in her absence! Enuma, did Ijem bite off your yam tendrils? *O ta biri gi ome ji,* Enuma?" she queried, wondering what had gone so wrong with her husband that he conducted himself so wickedly. "Imagine how worked up you are. Boiling for a little girl who is not even here? In case you don't know, Ijem, my daughter, is already in college, and that means she passed. My Ijem couldn't have failed. She is a daughter to be proud of. It's just a pity that you have refused to see the good in her. Your evil wishes will not prevail over good. Spare yourself the agony. She passed. Illiteracy and hatred have not allowed you to appreciate that little girl. She did not fail so stop celebrating," she said, and angrily left his presence when he threatened her to stop talking or he would descend on her as usual.

"I know that my Ijem will wipe my tears. I know she is a special child who will pull the plug off my misfortune, and longsuffering," Nneka smiled as she looked up fixing her gaze to the clouds. "God, thank you so very much. Please, perfect all that concerns Ijem." She made the sign of the cross just like the true Catholic she was.

Fourteen

Nneka's life continuously proved to be hell on earth. It became hotter as the days went by. Enuma got more complicated as the days passed. Even his little children became so afraid of his presence. He was heedless about them and their welfare. They always had momentary respite each time he was away, but the mere sight of him returning changed the atmosphere immediately; from cordial to hostile. He was tagged a big bully by his children. "I don't like our father. He does not behave like Izu's father. Izu's father would buy them biscuits each time he goes out. He also takes them for drives in his car and we will only be watching them drive past as they wave their hands at us. In fact, let me go and wait by the road to see if they will carry me when they are coming back from the church," Anene said. Anene was five years old and Enuma's only son. As he finished saying that, all the children, Anene, Nkem, Chioma and Ijeoma, ran out to the junction to wait for Izu's father. When they eventually got there, they all started jumping and shouting, "Carry me, carry me, carry me!" He screeched to a halt and picked all of them in addition to his three children who were already in the car. He drove them around further seeing their excitement and finally drove them to his compound from where the Enumas ran back home.

"How I wish Izu's daddy is our father," Ijeoma said fantasizing. Ijeoma was the eldest daughter of Enuma and had just turned eleven. What Ijeoma had voiced was how they always wished to swap fathers.

✵   ✵   ✵   ✵   ✵

Things became more complicated in Enuma's household. Nneka was now succumbing to all kinds of nudges. She was suspicious of her husband. She had debated and sought reasons why her husband would prefer to always maltreat her. One of those days, she fell victim to one of the most wicked gossips any married woman could hear, especially for someone who was so unsure of her man. Information swirling in the rumour mill reached her that Enuma had paid the dowry of a woman, whom they said had been married, and divorced three times to three different men. Nneka turned her nose up on hearing that. "I'm ready for war," she retorted. Still fuming, she asked aloud, even as there was no one in sight, "Where would she stay? It obviously won't be in this one room. I'm not bothered a wee bit about Enuma marrying another wife, that is, as long as he keeps her somewhere else," she said with a note of defiance.

True to the rumour, Enuma did bring another woman but based on Nneka's stand on the issue, the woman could not withstand the fire. She eventually ran away. In the course of time, Enuma adjusted to the reality of not being able to keep two women in the same room; and made another room out of the adjoining store, converting it to become his own room. Having achieved that he then brought back the woman. By that gesture, Nneka knew that her continued stay in the house had become ridiculous. She bided her time, waiting for the auspicious time to make her next move.

On this particular day, Enuma went out very early in the morning and returned with a man that Nneka knew as a land speculator. She observed as both men stood pointing at the only piece of land that was left for Enuma and his only brother. Nneka watched, and imagined what was going on, thinking, *I hope it is not what I am thinking? I hope Enuma is not planning to sell this land. He has already sold off many without anything to show for*

it. Determined in her spirit she thought further, *I will not watch him sell this one too. This land belongs to both of them, and it is the duty of the elder brother to share the land between him and his younger brother. I will do something about it,* she told herself determinedly.

Later in the evening, Nneka went to talk to Enuma about the land. "Enuma, there is something I will like to discuss with you," she said tentatively.

"What is it?" he snapped without even looking in her direction.

"I saw you with Ichie Ezego inspecting our land ..." she said, trailing off.

"And so? What is your business with that?" he asked her in a harsh and menacing tone.

"I didn't mean to get you upset, please. I was just thinking that since that is the only land left for you and your brother that you should not sell it, at least, not without consulting your brother. Remember you have sold many other parcels of land, yet you can't boast of anything you achieved with the money you realised from the sales!" she reminded him pointedly.

"Enough, woman! I say enough! Your opinion is not solicited here, so let me be." Nneka, sensing danger, left his presence, infuriated.

She talked to Onyeka, her husband's brother, about her husband's move. With his help, word was sent out immediately, especially in the circle of the *umunna*, Enuma's kinsmen, warning them not to buy any land from Enuma. "Should anyone disregard this information, and goes ahead to buy the land, such a person should consider his money lost." The alert on the land had had its effect, and a pay-off. That move effectively stalled the sale, saving the land but left Enuma clutching for straws, and very exasperated.

✲ ✲ ✲ ✲ ✲

Linking Nneka to the stalemate, Enuma vented his frustrations on her. He beat her up the more, and with so much vehemence! With the presence of the strange woman, and the constant beatings, Nneka reviewed her strategy and left the house with the children in tow, for good. Choosing to preserve her life and that of the children rather than sticking it out with a brute, like Enuma.

❧ *Fifteen* ❧

Well, it is obvious that I have no help. There is nobody capable of sending me to school, and since I can't find my father, I really do not have any other option, she soliloquised and cried as she decided to succumb to the pressure to get married.

"Big girl, Madam the Madam, I heard you are getting married! The news is on the lips of everyone," Chika said, when she bumped into Ijem at the marketplace.

Ijem, looking dejected, sighed, and said lamely, "They only paid the dowry on Saturday." As if that denied the fact that she was married.

"Who is the lucky man?" Chika asked, with a naughty giggle.

"He lives in Lagos," Ijem replied somberly.

"Hmm, is he a businessman?"

"I guess so, considering what they said; they claim he's into clearing and forwarding."

"What does that mean?" Chika asked.

"I don't know. Maybe, they clear things and move them forward … in fact, I really can't say what that kind of business entails," she said, sounding disinterested, and generally not feeling like continuing the conversation.

"Hmm … Whatever that means, but will you continue school over there?" Chika asked.

"My dear, I don't know yet. The man said I will continue

later," Ijem said.

"Why later? You are still young ... and I think this is the best time to do the school stuff," Chika suggested.

"Hmm, my sister, I don't care again. I am just there, watching things as they unfold. The only good thing for which I am really happy about, is the fact that I will continue to stay with my grandmother until I am officially wedded," she offered, comforting herself. "So that will still give me the sense that I am still my normal self, and not pushed to feeling like I am already a housewife," she added.

"Take it easy, my dear. Meanwhile, congratulations again!" Chika said, patting Ijem on her back as they hugged very tightly.

"Please, save that congratulation for the time when it would be needed. I don't really see the need now," Ijem said in a raspy voice, as they went their separate ways.

Ijem eventually completed her SS3 when the strike was called off. She was now able to pay for her West African Senior Secondary Certificate Examination (WASSCE) and National Examination Council (NECO) from the savings she made from her petty business activities, and the financial help she got from Jack, her betrothed husband, who was forced on her.

She prepared the much she could because she practically had skipped most parts of her SS2 due to the protracted strike. The students only took the promotion examinations and jumped straight into the next class–SS3. She attended the few classes that were available, staying in the boarding house for four months, which was the rule in their school. SS3 students were mandated to spend the final year class in the boarding house to enable them to be well prepared for the external examinations.

She made the best of those four months given her impoverished state. Savouring every moment, knowing that that opportunity may be her only chance of living, and experiencing life in a school environment. She had come to school as a day-student all through her junior school days.

Soon the WASSCE and NECO examinations came and were done with, and the SS3 students were sent off from secondary school. *This seems like the climax of my education. Well, God I thank you at least for making me complete my SS3 education. No matter how incomplete the strike had made it to appear,* Ijem thought to herself, half-pleased with her educational accomplishment so far. "The only downside is this so-called betrothal that I have been forced into accepting," she muttered, self-deprecatingly.

Having graduated fresh from secondary school and with nothing more to do, Ijem spent all her time at home helping her grandmother, Nnedimma; either in the farm, or with her *ugba* business or the regular house chores.

One fateful day, Chuka, her uncle, came home for a few days from Port Harcourt where he lived. He was Nnedimma's first son, who was just recently settled after completing his apprenticeship.

On this lovely evening, as Ijem would like to recall, something good happened. "Nne," Chuka called out even as he started saying, "I will like Ijem to come and spend some time with me since Chiazo has come back now. I learnt that Ijem has never been anywhere outside this village. At least you'll have someone to stay with while she is away," he said breathlessly. Eavesdropping on the conversation, Ijem could not contain her joy. She had spent the whole of the day since her uncle returned pleading with him to take her to Port Harcourt, which incidentally would be her first time of getting out of the village. He had assured her that he'll talk to his mother but needed time to consider the matter before doing so. Emerging from behind the compound, Ijem interjected their conversation. "Nne, don't worry, Ijeoma will also come to stay with you before I come back," she said, reassuring her grandmother about her welfare even in her impending absence.

✻   ✻   ✻   ✻   ✻

Ijem boarded a mini-bus to Port Harcourt, and for the first time, to spend some time with her uncle, Chuka.

✻   ✻   ✻   ✻   ✻

Chuka's business was not yet flourishing but the joy of being the owner and the master of his own business kept him looking forward to the future and what it held for the growth of the trade that he had spent the last five years learning.

They arrived Chuka's one-bedroom apartment after spending five hours on the road. It was exciting for Ijem. Uncle Chuka opened the door, and asked Ijem to step inside as he said, "Welcome to my humble abode." Ijem cast quick glances around the room; her first observation was the medium-sized television and radio set that were placed atop a little table sitting at the right corner of the room.

There was also a cramped-up bed and a mattress neatly resting atop it. The floor was covered with a red rug. Everything felt different from what Ijem had ever been exposed to. It was a luxuriant scenario, given where she was coming from.

Later in the evening when they had settled in, and were watching television, Chuka said to Ijem, "I love the intelligence you show and your clear hunger for education. I will help you the much I can. But I must warn you that I have nothing yet. You know that I am just starting life after my period of apprenticeship. I am working hard, hoping that the future will be bright."

"Thank you, Uncle," Ijem said. Her joy knew no bounds. She was not perturbed by the lack or was it the near bankruptcy that her uncle had just confessed, but her joy was based on his expressed willingness to support her education. A very wonderful development. These were good intentions.

Leveraging on the mood of the moment, Ijem said, "Uncle, can I get a Joint Admission and Matriculations' Board (JAMB) form when the registration starts?"

After a moment, her uncle asked, "When will that be?"

"I think that will be sometime in January, Uncle."

"Okay! No problem. Tell me when the time comes. I know I can afford a JAMB form for now," Chuka said enthusiastically.

"Thank you, Uncle," Ijem said, smiling.

With that promise, Ijem started studying for the JAMB examination. Chuka, her uncle taught her how to operate the electronics in the house–the TV and the radio sets. She was overwhelmed with joy at acquiring the little knowledge.

Ijem spent four months in Port Harcourt before Christmas. "When are you travelling for Christmas, Ijem?" Chuka inquired waiting for her response.

"Uncle, it depends on you now."

"Okay, as for me, I will be travelling on December 27, but I suppose you may want to spend the Christmas at home. In that case, you will get ready to travel on the 19th. But we can both return together if you don't mind spending the Christmas here in Port Harcourt?"

"Okay, Uncle," she responded excitedly, not minding what date it was that they would travel.

Ijem travelled on the 19th as scheduled. Surprisingly, Chuka returned on the 24th. It appeared as if loneliness had chased him out of Port Harcourt. But not so, he came back feverish and two days later, Chuka started hiccupping. An experience that would ordinarily be stopped by drinking water. But the hiccupping persisted even after he had taken several litres of water.

Apparently his situation had gone beyond what could be contained by the fabled water therapy. They tried several hospitals to stop his debilitating condition to no avail. In the first week of January, he was taken to a herbalist who gave him some herbal medicine. Minutes later, Chuka vomitted what looked like two live vegetable maggots, traditionally called *obubuo*. To every body's surprise and chagrin, the herbalist said that Chuka was poisoned.

All along even before Ijem came to Port Harcourt to stay with him, he had always treated himself for malaria, typhoid fever and other ailments as was suggested by the doctors yet he remained sick.

"Praise God," was on the lips of every member of Nnedimma's immediate family. Chuka himself sang and danced in happiness. Two weeks after the incident, he returned to Port Harcourt promising to send the money for Ijem's JAMB examination.

Ijem was sitting on the pavement, in front of the left room in their mud house when Jack came, stepping into the compound in his usual bouncy manner. "Mama, how are you today?" he said as he exchanged pleasantries with Nnedimma.

"I thought you people were supposed to leave today?" Nnedimma said, looking up at him with raised brows, inquiringly.

"Yes, Ma, but I couldn't make it as planned. I will travel in the next two days."

"Oh, I see," Nnedimma said, nodding understandably. Jack went over to his wife.

"Good evening, Sir."

"Good evening, my dear and how are you?" he inquired.

"Fine," Ijem said tersely. He had observed how withdrawn Ijem had become since her return from Port Harcourt. He thought quickly of what to do to pull her out of whatever it was that was the matter.

Jack tickled her fancy when he suddenly said, "I have a surprise for you, Ijem." Her heart skipped a beat as her imagination ran riot, making her to wonder what the surprise could be. *Could he have changed his mind, and now wants to support my education?* she tried to guess. The thought of that happening made her suddenly flash a beautiful smile at him and continue to stare at him expectantly for him to quickly say what the surprise was. Not getting a quick response, she asked him a barrage of questions.

"Please, what is the surprise? What is it? Is it my JAMB examination?"

Jack turned his face away from her, and then spun and squatted as he gently dragged her to sit. He stared at her thoughtfully, exhaled deeply and started to say something to her in a low and deeply modulated tone: "Ijem, it's something better than that." Disappointed, she looked the other way. She got up, took a few steps toward the *ugiri* tree in the compound, a very big and an economic tree that provided shade in the compound. The fruit, the *ugiri* itself, served as food and also a means of income. The seed was used in making the popular *ogbono* soup. Leaning on the tree, she stayed there gazing vacantly into the air. Jack followed, stood looking at her face as he tried to explain. "I'll want you to start up a business, Ijem. This will be good for you and Mama. We shall also be making some good money from that business so that we can *concrude our malliage lites*" (conclude our marriage rites), he said, not minding how his heavy Igbo accent interfered with his spoken English.

Jack had already constructed a kiosk for her phone call and recharge card business and had merely come to inform her about it. She managed to conceal her displeasure. After a week of brooding over the issue, she accepted to do the business. She sold recharge cards and offered phone call services, where people would pay to make and receive calls with her phone. She later on added the renting of home videos and other related businesses.

In no time she developed a clientele which included a network of priests and a couple of other persons who could buy recharge cards from her from wherever they were. It was an unspoken agreement between her and the customers. They voluntarily did that to encourage her. They would pay up anytime she wanted to replenish her stock. The business flourished. She was making quite some money. At least she did not have to walk about, hawking sundry articles of trade under the sun or rain.

Her husband went about bragging and announcing to every ear that cared to listen how he started the business for his wife. What he did not tell them was how little the start-up capital was, and how his wife-to-be had managed to turn it into what it had become.

She continued doing the business while she waited for the JAMB registration which was supposed to commence in two weeks.

Ijem was at her business spot when her business phone rang; it was her uncle's close friend in Port Harcourt. At the second ring, she picked up the call. "Hello, hello," came the response from the other end of the phone, "this is Nnamdi."

"Brother Nnamdi, good afternoon," Ijem replied.

"How are you doing, Ijem?"

"I am fine, Brother,"

"Okay, Ijem, could you send me Emeka's number. The number of your uncle that lives in Lagos?"

Funnily, her heart skipped a beat. "Brother, I hope there is no problem?" she managed to ask.

"No problem at all. I just wanted him to help me send down my goods through courier."

"Okay. I will forward his number. Is this your number?"

"Yes. Okay then, I'll be waiting for it," he said.

"Bro, bro ... bro please, hold on, wait a minute, could you

help me tell Uncle Chuka to call me today? Tell him that Mama wants to speak with him. She has been worried about him especially since he went back to Port Harcourt. In fact, she wanted to send Chiazo to come and check on him."

"Okay, I will, but didn't he come home?"

"Which home again? He's in Port Harcourt now? But how do you mean? Did he tell you he would come home recently?"

"No, not really. Don't worry, I will deliver your message when I see him," he said dropping the call.

"Mama, don't worry. It's late already. It's 9 pm. Go to bed. First thing tomorrow morning, I will set out to Port Harcourt. I will go and check on him but I assure you that he is fine. Chiazo assured Nnedimma.

"Oh … Please o, go and check on my son o."

"Mama, please eat your food please," pleaded Ijem. "You have not eaten since afternoon."

"I am not hungry, my daughter, all I want is to see Chuka nwam. Something tells me he is not alright."

"Mama, I have told you to stop worrying. I will travel to Port Harcourt tomorrow since we can't reach him through any of his friends yet," Chiazo said with a sense of irritation.

"Please, take it easy on her…" cautioned Ijem. "I spoke with Bro Nnamdi today, I told him to tell Bro Chuka to call me. But he asked if he visited home. I only wondered why he asked that?"

"Hey!!! Chuka my son…oooo," Nnedimma wailed. "I hope you are fine wherever you are now."

"Mama, he is fine please."

Very early that Eke market day. Chiazo was set to leave for Port Harcourt but he had to help Nnedimma convey her *ugba* and other goods to the market with the wheel barrow. After dropping her goods off at the market, he set out to gather fruits that he would take to his brother in Port Harcourt. Ijem as well was already at her business stand as usual.

Her phone rang, she quickly picked it up as if she was expecting someone.

"Hello, Ijem," came a rather depressed voice from the other end.

"Yes, who is speaking?"

"Agu."

"Ah, Bro, is everything okay. You don't sound cheerful. Please, did you see my brother recently? Do you know if he is okay?"

"That is why I called, Ijem."

"Yes, Bro," she responded anxiously.

"What was that course you said you want to study in the university?"

She paused for a few seconds wondering why he asked that question. "Medicine," she responded faintly. "Bro why do you ask? What does it have to do with my brother?" she thought, Could it be that Bro Chuka is no longer willing to support my education?

"That means you want to be a doctor?"

"Yes, Bro."

"And what is a doctor's job?"

"Ah ah, Bro, why all these questions?"

"Answer me, Ijem," he demanded.

"Okay, doctors treat patients."

"When they don't succeed what happens?"

"Bro, what is all these now? What are these questions about? Talk to me, Bro. What is happening? Is my brother okay?" she queried as her legs wobbled.

"Ijem, calm down and answer my question."

"Okay, the patient dies," she said almost losing her breath.

"Ijem, there is nothing the eyes would see and shed blood, there is nothing too boisterous for the ear to hear, there is nothing new under the sun. Please, take heart, my dear. Chuka your brother is dead!" There was a bombshell. At least it sounded so in Ijem's ears. "He died in an accident ..." The words 'Chuka your brother is dead' resonated in her ears and memories. She became voiceless. She could not say a word. She wanted to talk but remained breathless and voiceless ... until a few seconds later.

Rivers of tears flowed freely down her cheeks. "Do not hang up, Ijem," Agu demanded. But the phone was no longer on her ear as he tried to explain what happened. "He was to be a best man to his friend that was to wed tomorrow but he travelled for his medical check-up and has not returned till now. It happened that he was involved in an accident that claimed his life and none of the other passengers was hurt. Take heart, please. It's really a pity, your brother from Lagos is already here as he was contacted last night, take heart, Ijem. Please, accept my condolences." The phone disconnected.

Ijem felt like giving up the ghost. "Hey! Why my brother? Why Bro Chuka? Hey! God, where are you? Why do you let bad things happen? Ewoooo!!!! Mama eee!!! Bro Chuka ee!!!" she paused, held herself, took a deep breath ... looked around her. Suddenly, she sprang up on her feet, cast glances around the kiosk as if looking for Chuka. "No, this is not true. This cannot be true now. It's not true. Bro Chuka will send money for my JAMB next week. He promised to do that so how can he die?"

Just then Chiazo stopped by, announcing his departure for Port Harcourt but noticed she was crying. She broke the bad news to him. He was as hit as Ijem. He stood still as if confused. He asked the same questions Ijem asked. "How, how come? Who told you?" He sat at the door of the kiosk for minutes, tears streamed down his cheeks. He was deeply touched. But he managed to pull himself together when he thought about his mother and how she would take the news. He rallied round and conveyed Nneka on a motorcycle down to the house. He also reached out to Nnedimma's only surviving brother, Nnabuike; they gathered to devise the best way to break the sad news to Nnedimma, to avoid a crisis.

They made series of promises to Nnedimma in a bid to stabilise her and keep her soul from exiting with her son's. 'The only hope for the family' Nnedimma wept bitterly, her body trembled. She grieved so hard. She almost died in the process.

Unfortunately, he didn't live to fulfil his promise. He died in a ghastly motor accident along Port Harcourt-Owerri road. Ijem's dream of going to a higher institution again came crashing before her very eyes.

She cried profusely. She wept bitterly. She asked questions. *Why is my own different? Is it that my creator has no plan for me in this world? Why does any light of opportunity on my way get dimmed in a twinkle? What exactly does He want me to do? What should I do?* She prepared and read a very touchy oration at the funeral of her uncle, Chuka. The end of the funeral marked a great drawback for Ijem.

⌘ Sixteen ⌘

One month after the burial, Ijem went back to her business. It dawned on her that yes, it may not be the will of the creator for her to proceed to a higher institution. She wore a black upon black dress or white upon white daily for three months using that as a mark of respect and mourning for her uncle who had given her so much to hope and dream about. She carried on her life like a moving empty vessel. She jettisoned every thought, dream or wish of ever going to school. She accepted her situation as a done deal. She had accepted her situation as normal until one day when her dream came staring at her again.

On that day, two ladies came to make phone calls at her phone booth. One of the girls had a book that had the shape and size of a foreign novel. While her friend was dialing a number to call, Ijem seized the opportunity to ask her friend for a favour. "Please, can I take a look at the book?" stretching out her hand to receive the book.

The girl rather held back the book from her saying, "Sorry, it's not for your level," smirking with some level of contempt. Ijem was rather taken aback by her rudeness. She tried to ignore the rude remark and still demanded.

"Please, can I just take a look?" The girl reluctantly handed the book to her. It was titled *Physiology*. "What course are you studying?" Ijem asked.

"Pharmacy," the girl replied, rolling her eyes and shaking her head in that girlish manner. Ijem ignored her little drama and followed up with another question.

"And your friend?"

"Same!" the spoilt brat spat out.

"What level?"

"300 level!" she replied irritably.

"Which school?"

"UniBen and please e-xcu-se me!" the girl dragged, twisting her neck and body as if doing a break dance. That finally put paid to the conversation.

"Okay, that's nice and congratulations," Ijem said, taking the cue. They paid her for the service and walked away, chatting and laughing. Ijem watched them until they disappeared around the corner. Ijem's eyes misted as she drifted into a depressive mood. *I should have been in the university now, studying Pharmacy or Medicine. Imagine the insults! If I had been an undergraduate, would that girl have said all that? Oh God! Why can't I go to the university? Why can't I be like these girls? Why must it be my lot to marry at this stage when I have not achieved any academic milestone?*

She broke down in tears. She squatted on the floor in her kiosk, closed the door for business, and sulked as though her life depended on how long she cried.

Barely one week after her encounter with the UniBen girls, another young lady came to make a phone call at her booth. While talking on the phone, the girl talked a lot about an examination. As usual, it stirred Ijem's interest. She latched on what she had overheard her say on phone and anxiously asked while collecting the phone from her, "Please, which examination were you talking about?"

The lady instead of responding to her harmless question rather took a very contemptuous look at her and chuckled. She went around Ijem as if she was inspecting her dress. After her sniggering inspection, she queried her malevolently, "Why are you asking ask me that kind of question? Are you here to eavesdrop on people's telephone conversations, and proceed to ask them stupid questions? What's your problem? Plea...se! Take your money." She grabbed her hand and slapped the money into her palm, turned and strode away. Ijem could not believe her eyes. With arms akimbo, she watched in amazement as the belligerent girl disappeared from her sight. Myriads of thoughts enveloped her mind and she fell into another bout of depression.

✻   ✻   ✻   ✻   ✻

The two encounters with the girls left her in sheer misery. She kept vigil at nights as there was nobody to share her burden with. She would go through her WASSCE results and cry even more. She would pray amidst tears, "God, my result can fetch me many courses in the university. My only impediment is money for the fees," she drifted off and slept with her results under her pillow (made up of a pack of clothes). She wept so often; her heart was so burdened and heavy one night that she picked up her phone, went out under the *ugiri* tree and put a call through to a Catholic Reverend Father, Fr. Emeka. The father was the priest in charge of the local church where she worshipped.

"Father, good evening!"

"Ijem, are you okay? Is everything alright with you? You are crying. What is the problem?"

"Father, I want to go to school, I want to go to school," she said repeatedly. He paused for some seconds. He had flashes of thoughts of how many times he had discussed school issues with her. She had even suggested going to a computer school so as to assuage her urge for a university education. He recalled having advised her to check her business peak times so that she can decide what time of the day to attend the classes.

After a few seconds of reflection, he said, "Ijem, I want you to mark this date. The same way you called me this night crying that you want to go to school, so will you call me in no distant time to tell me you have an admission."

"Father, how is that possible?" she murmured over the phone.

"Ijem, do you believe that all things are possible with our creator?"

"Yes, Father."

"Good, then have faith. Silver and gold, I have none to give you but I trust the Almighty I serve to grant your good heart's desire. It shall be well with you, Ijem. He will take care of your needs. Weep no more, my dear."

"Thank you, Father!"

"Sleep well!" the Rev. Fr. said, as he dropped the phone.

The business of selling recharge cards continued. It had been six months since Chuka was buried. Ijem decided to face life as it presented itself.

"Good afternoon, Sir, she greeted a customer who stopped his car to buy a recharge card from her. She noticed it was the same man who had bought many recharge cards from her in the morning. She was happy because the man had bought the highest denominations of recharge cards. Why are you not in school?" the man asked as he was recharging the credit he just bought from her.

"I have finished secondary school, Sir."

"Don't you have plans of going to a higher institution?" the man asked pointedly. She did not know the right thing to say. He asked again, "You don't want to proceed to a higher institution?"

"I want to, Sir, but I can't."

"You can't? Why?" he asked, staring at her. Her eyes became misty as she mumbled.

"My family cannot afford to sponsor me to a higher

institution, Sir."

"I see. Well, Just keep an open mind, okay. You strike me as an industrious young girl, and you sound quite intelligent too. Where did you grow up?"

"In this village."

With a look of surprise written all over him, he said, "This village?" She nodded. "That's interesting! Don't worry. Pray, I believe in miracles or should we say providence?"

"Thank you, Sir."

Suddenly the man asked her, "How much do you get a dozen of ₦1,500 recharge cards here?"

"It's ₦13,750 naira, Sir."

"Okay, when I get back to Lagos, I will buy and send you some airtime so you can add to your stock."

"Thank you, Sir. God bless you." He paid and drove off.

He returned shortly, Ijem ran out at the sound of a horn thinking he wanted more recharge cards but surprisingly he offered her fifteen thousand naira! She was taken aback. She was afraid to collect the money as she ruminated in her heart: *Who is this man and why is he being this nice to me? Hmmm! Maybe I would turn into a vulture, a pussycat, tortoise or just any other thing if I should touch this money. This could be a ritualist.* Her mind wandered. "No, thank you, Sir! I can't take that."

"Just take this. I decided instead of waiting till I get back to Lagos, I should just give you the money to augment your business. I don't mean any harm. I just want to encourage you. Don't be afraid. I am your brother. I am from this village. My house is down the road. I am of the Nneobi family. Do you know Nneobi family?"

"Yes, Sir! But I don't know the members of the family. I only know the family house."

"Very good, now you know I am your brother. Take the

money."

Ijem closed her eyes as she collected the money believing she may just disappear to somewhere else. But amazingly, she opened her eyes and saw that she was still in front of her shop. She grinned.

"Thank you, Sir. God bless you and replenish your pocket a billion folds. I am very grateful, Sir!" She continued in her prayerful wishes as the man drove off. She waved till the car vanished from her sight. She went back to her kiosk. She spent reasonable time inspecting the notes with serious thoughts and imaginations running through her mind. She could not wait to break the news to her grandmother. She would have just run home to tell her but she was expected to fetch fodder for the goats.

❧ *Seventeen* ❧

With that financial boost, Ijem concentrated fully on her business. She made more connection of customers. Priests connected their fellow priests to patronise her as a way of encouraging her. She had been very active in church activities. She represented the church in quiz competitions at the Deanery and Diocesan levels. She became the president of her Block Rosary Crusade from the age of ten when she returned from Enuma's house to her grandmother. She had always given her best in any activity she got involved in. She was an instructor at Catechism classes from the age of thirteen. Her consistency with church activities and doggedness to make a difference endeared her to many priests from that young age. She was naturally known by seminarians who were sent to the parish on apostolic work.

Her tie to the church attracted a few more priest customers to her business. She kept busy while trying to assimilate the reality of her plight.

One fateful day, Ijem was on her way returning from the communication stores at Onitsha where she usually replenished her stock when she had an encounter which changed the way things were working out for her. A young man with a foreign accent walked up to her as she was striding to get on to ride on an *okada*.

In the most humble manner, the young man said, "Please,

Sister, I am looking for this address," he flashed a piece of paper. Leaning closer, he said, "It's number 20 Omaliko street, Onitsha." Naïve and unbeknown to her, she was being sucked into what had been the rave of the moment in Onitsha. Ijem stopped in her tracks and got curious to take a closer look at the address the young man was holding so close to himself.

"Okay," she said. "There is a place called Omaliko joint. I think this is the way..." as she pointed north, but said, "but I don't really know. I suggest you ask those people going to the main market, they may know." She made a few steps to continue on her way to the *okada* park, when the same person excused her again.

"Please, I am a foreigner. I am from Cameroon. I don't know anywhere. At the hotel I lodged in last night, I was robbed of all my dollars. Now, I only hope to get to my client so that I can make my supply and collect my money. If not, I will be stuck and I don't know how to go about selling these goods on my own. I don't speak English so well. L'argon, c'est finis!"

"Ehya!" she exclaimed pitifully. "How I wish I know where the place is but I don't. Just ask these business people. I am sure they may know the place." She stepped forward while looking at the man, askance, and at the same time empathising with his predicament. Just then a shorter man walked towards her as if shadowing her.

Approaching her closely, he asked, "What was that man telling you?"

Surprised at what his concern was with what transpired between her and the other man, Ijem grimaced saying, "Do I know you? And what is your business with what he said to me?"

"Sorry, just that the man talked to me too. He said he was robbed!" Just then, her heart melted on hearing that again as she pondered awhile.

"I wonder why our people would treat a foreigner like that. I think it's so unfair. They even beat him up too. Chai!" She turned to steal a glance and saw the man strolling aimlessly. "He does not

116

even speak English well. I wish I knew the place he was looking for. I would have just helped him. It's really sad," Ijem contemplated.

"We can help him. Our sales girl in the office ran into one of these same foreigners last month who complained of having been robbed in the street and after helping them, she was handsomely rewarded. They gave her a hair dryer and some other appliances. Now she is no longer working with us. She has opened her own salon."

"Are you serious? But the problem is that I don't even know the exact address of where he is looking for. It's not even about what I can gain. If I knew the place, I would have told him immediately, so he can go and get his money and go back to his country in one piece. If you know the place just direct him now," she urged him.

"We can help him!"

Just as she was finishing, the foreigner joined them, pleading, "Please, just help me and distribute what I have, let me just realise enough money to go back to my country. Please, my sister!"

Yet contemplating what to do, Ijem hesitated for a moment. "I think we should just go and see what kind of goods you have," the second man who had just introduced himself as Kelechi, suggested. Whether out of pity or crass naivety, or for some other reason, Ijem followed them without further resistance. On their way to the place, the foreigner introduced himself as Lucas. He talked to Ijem in confidence, speaking in French. "My sister, *'Je suis ton frère maintenant. Je n'ai pas parles bien l'anglais.'* Meaning: I don't speak English fluently. *'J 'ai besoin de….'*" Ijem interrupted.

"Please, I don't understand all these French you are speaking. Try and say whatever it is, anyhow, in English, I will try and understand."

"I trust you, Sister. Help me, *si'l te plait.*"

"We are already going to see if we can help you. It's a pity

117

what happened to you last night. Everything will be fine," she consoled Lucas as they walked. "All Nigerians are not armed robbers. I hope you won't have this as a lasting impression of our country." She tried to correct the impression of his ordeal in the hands of robbers.

"Wait here! Let's bring out the goods," said Lucas and Kelechi.

Ijem waited patiently along with a third boy that had joined Kelechi on their way. After a while, Kelechi and Lucas returned holding in their hands a sachet of water, a brand of detergent and a wad of papers that looked as if it was cut from a light brown-coloured envelop. "This is what he said he came with!" Kelechi said, holding out the wad of papers for all to see. "He said he didn't even know what was in there. It was his father's consignment to a client in Onitsha. His father, he said, sent it from Switzerland. Now, it's apparent that this is fortune for all of us," Kelechi enthused. "Just watch out!" Kelechi added. Ijem watched curiously with Lucas and the last boy who claimed to be Ifeanyi. Kelechi held out the paper for all to see to assure all of them that it was the only thing he was holding. He cut open the sachet of water with his teeth. Poured water on the paper and started washing it with the detergent. To their amazement, the cleaned up paper turned out to be a five hundred naira note. Ijem was astonished.

"So this is how they print our money? Jeez!" Others also appeared to be equally shocked at this revelation.

"Wait, wait, wait!" Kelechi cautioned. "I know that we are all excited about this, but this kind of excitement is also dangerous. Not just for us but to this business. Since we have seen that we are about to be blessed beyond understanding, we are going to take an oath to enable us protect this secret. That oath will help to seal our lips so we don't get into unnecessary trouble. The procedure is simple," Kelechi continued. He then told them to spit into their palms. They all did. He started talking gibberish. The only part that Ijem heard clearly was when he said, "If I will die when I divulge what we are about doing here, let this saliva on my palm appear at the back my palms." They all repeated what he had told them to say and to their utmost surprise, the saliva in their palms mysteriously appeared at the back of their palms.

Ijem's eyes bulged out in shock. "Oh my God!" she screamed.

"Hey!" Lucas even screamed in disbelief, with his hands on his head. "I never knew that was what I had; *Mon pere* did not specify what was there. Sometimes he does business with *Mbanjo-Mbanjo, TinuTinu, Kenekuku, Atika-Atrta* and others. I didn't know it was all about *l'argon du Nigerian. Mon pere a' habites a la Suisse.* My father lives in Switzerland."

Kelechi interrupted him, saying, "He didn't know that his father does business from Switzerland with some Nigerian leaders, and some elites. He prints and sends Nigerian currency from Switzerland. But you know this is a business that can change somebody's status overnight. So his father concealed it from him. We are lucky to unravel this with him. He is willing to share everything equally with us. But we have a problem now!" he paused. "This money is still in packets of films, and we need chemical to wash them clean into real money. The problem now is that, the only place we can get this film is from a teaching hospital. That is the kind of film they use for X-rays. It is imported from America or London, so we cannot buy it from any other place." He paused and observed their faces contorted in deep thoughts and burning anxiety. Satisfied, he knew that he had captured their interests. "They are of different denominations," he continued. "We all would need to contribute money to actualise the transformation of the films into real money. Everybody here will contribute and we would keep a record of our contributions. The minute we finish the printing, we would first refund everybody to the tune of his or her contributions. So let's run around and raise some money," he said.

❦‖ *Eighteen* ‖❦

Having been sucked into the drama, Ijem decided to give the venture a chance. And since she had no other money left as she had just bought recharge cards when she met Lucas, she thought quickly to return to where she bought the cards to plead with them for a refund of the twenty thousand naira she paid. "I got home and met my grandmother sick. We need money to pay for her treatment. Please, if you wouldn't mind giving me that money back to me," she lied.

The agent that usually sold recharge cards to her sympathised with her and returned the twenty thousand naira to her. "You can go with the money and the cards, after selling the cards, you can come and pay. Take it easy!" Ijem gladly collected the money and returned to her new business partners. They collected the money and even the recharge cards, and exchanged phone numbers with her. Kelechi and Ifeanyi left for the Teaching Hospital with her money and the recharge cards on the promise that others had equally contributed their own money although she did not sight their contributions and did not think anything was amiss either. Ijem and Lucas waited for hours under a big tree.

When they eventually returned, Kelechi who was sweating, told them a story instead of reporting strictly on what transpired at the hospital. "You needed to have seen this accident that just happened around Oba junction. A trailer hauling cement ran over a car carrying a pregnant woman. The woman was badly injured and bleeding so much. She was unconscious when she was brought into the hospital. Oh! It was quite a disgusting and pitiable sight. So the doctor only managed to tell us the price of the film before the emergency call came in. He collected the money we had as a deposit, to show that we are serious. He said he would have to order for more from London. He said half a litre is five hundred thousand naira. The money we gave him can barely afford a spoon of the chemical. So we need to raise more money. Ijem almost burst into tears out of pity for the imaginary pregnant woman that was involved in an accident and partly for her business. She left in the evening without even enough transport fare.

That was the beginning of trouble for Ijem. The partners continued to demand for more money from Ijem, telling her one story today and another one tomorrow. She borrowed from her customers till she parted with eighty-eight thousand naira for the *wash-wash* business with her partners. She had believed: *soon, I will get my own share of the money. I will take from it and pay my fees in the university. Take my grandmother to the hospital so they can permanently cure her of the sickness that has disturbed her all my life. I will give my mum and all my uncles enough money to start good businesses. I will pay my sibling's school fees too.*

One of the days after meeting with her partners to deposit what she had gathered, and on her way back home, she stopped by somewhere. There were a lot of men there; fathers, young men, boys, all waiting for jobs. It turned out to be a pool of workers of some sorts; plumbers, masons, electricians, painters and all kinds of artisans. She regarded them with some pity. In her mind, she said when I get this money, I will come here and help them. Should I pick a few of them and give them huge sums of money to start their own businesses so they can help others too or should I just give all of them fifty thousand naira each? Ijem would stop in front of any beautiful edifice she passed by and enquire about the cost of the building and cost of furnishing such a house. She was looking for and imagining the kind of house she would build in her grandmother's place and for her mother when she gets her share of the money.

✡ ✡ ✡ ✡ ✡

Days and weeks passed and until the fourth week. Ijem ran out of patience. She had no money to run her business again. She had started becoming leaner and unkempt. She called Kelechi. "Please, I want to see you."

"I hope there is no problem?"

"There is no problem. It's just that I think this is taking too long. When are we expecting the chemical?"

"Ah, ah! You know our problem. We still don't have enough money to buy the chemical" Kelechi reminded her.

"Please, let's get the quantity of chemical that the money we have contributed so far can fetch, so that we can print some money and then take part of the money printed to pay for more chemicals," she suggested.

"Oyibo people don't do things like that! They can even get the police involved if we show desperation. They may even nab us. In fact, I want to change my line so that the police cannot trace us. As soon as I change the line, I will call you with my new line. But if you have any money, let's meet at the same location." She exploded out of frustration. "Which money again? I am so broke, I don't even have cards to sell again and you are talking about more money. See, I have put in eighty-eight thousand naira into this."

"Ehn! Do you know how much I have put in myself?"

"Yes, tell me! How much have you contributed?

Wait, how much is remaining to reach the target?"

"We still need two hundred and fifty thousand naira."

"Oh my God! Serious?"

"See, just relax, we are almost there, Ifeanyi has travelled to Lagos to collect some money. When he returns, we will know how much we have. You know Lucas is not contributing anything. In fact, I have been feeding him all this while. But then, not to worry I will deduct all these expenses. Relax, it will be over soon."

"Okay." She dropped the call.

Kelechi and partners never called nor responded to her calls from that day. At a point, the lines became permanently unavailable. It then dawned on her that she had been duped. She wept bitterly and could not even tell anyone because of the oath that she was forced to take.

That was how she got into a big debt. One of her customers granted her a relief. Business was no longer as good as it used to be due to lack of funds to replenish her stock. She kept tottering. It even affected her welfare and led her into skipping her meals. Sometimes, she starved herself in the name of fasting to see whether she could make up for her stupidity. She regretted succumbing to help Lucas. She hated Kelechi. *Those were fake names after all, and I'd believed we were in that business for real. Coming at a time that I desperately needed money for my education in the university. But I had been lured into the business believing that all of us were in it genuinely. But they were all the same, and in that dubious group. They will surely face their punishment for duping me out of what I call innocent greed and naivety. I never knew such exists. Such phantoms! How could I have been so stupid? And now, about that oath. Is it true? But how did the saliva manage to appear behind my palms. Hmmm! That must be magic. That shows it's true. God please save me from this kind of trouble.* She mulled.

Ijem suffered more during this period. Her heart was burdened with so much sorrow that she could not even discuss it with anyone. She wore a very pronounced lean and hungry look. The skirts she wore became loose on her waist to the extent that she would have to tie them to her waist with a rope. Since she had no belt except the white school belt she used as a student, she preferred wearing her gowns which were now oversized. She wept every night. She regretted and cursed the day she met Lucas, Kelechi and Ifeanyi. She prayed for God's vengeance on them. She cursed them relentlessly.

Ijem started paying off her debts gradually. It became yet another trying period in her life ... a continuous ellipsis, a short way around her life. She put in every kobo she got trying to get back her business to the level it was.

⟨ꙅ∥ *Nineteen* ∥ꙅ⟩

After the encounter she had with Lucas, she started buying and renting home videos and musical videos. Soon she got back to her usual business spirit but with more wisdom. She continued building and maintaining her network of priestly customers. The priests patronised her not just because they could always visit her stand but because she could send the recharge cards they needed via short message service (SMS). When making payments the priests would normally give her extra money in excess of the cost of the SMS and the recharge cards.

One evening, she had very low stock and needed to replenish her stock but was short of cash. She put a call through to one of the priests who owed her but lived in a parish in the neighbouring town.

"Good evening, Father, it's me, Ijem. Please, I will need money so I can replenish my stock."

"Okay, Ijem. Could you please do me a favour?"

"What is it, Father?"

"I will be travelling to Port Harcourt in the morning, meaning I will be unable to get the money across to you. But I will drop your money with the gateman. Don't worry; I will add money for your transport expenses. You can come and pick your money."

"Okay, Father, which of the parishes is that, and how do I get there?"

"I will text the address of the parish to you. Thanks and have a good evening."

The next morning, she prepared to go to the parish but got a call informing her that her school mother had a stillbirth. So she went to commiserate with her. By the time she got to the parish, it was evening and so the priest had returned and retrieved the money from the gateman.

While she was approaching the parish house, another priest drove in, parked and responded to Ijem's greetings as he walked past her.

"Please, come up," Father Uche beckoned on her with a wave of his hands. She went up and met the same priest that passed her at the lobby. "This is our international communications minister," he joked. "Call her up anytime of the day and you will have any type of recharge card you want." Father Uche introduced Ijem to the other priest he referred to as Father Mmaduka.

"That is very good," Father Mmaduka said as he looked at her.

Father Uche gave her the money he owed. Returned some videos he had rented. Father Mmaduka went through the videos, and took a musical video and offered to buy it but did not pay for it immediately. It was on credit. She left. It had increased her network of customers by one. Father Mmaduka patronised her so much and would pay her through the parish cook because he was not always around at the times she usually went for her money.

One day, she was lucky to meet him and the following transpired during the encounter.

"How are you, and how is your business going?"

"I am fine, Father, and the business is fine," Ijem said bashfully.

"How long have you been doing this business?"

"About eight months now," Ijem said.

"Why are you not in school?"

"I have finished my secondary school."

"Ehn! Meaning you don't want to continue to the university?" She held her breath. "I'd wanted to but I cannot."

"You cannot? How do you mean?" the Reverend Father asked. She paused, fixed her gaze on the floor, her elbow resting on the arm rest while supporting her left cheek with her left hand. He observed the change in her countenance and urged her to speak. "Talk to me. Tell me about it, Ijem." She explained everything, leaving out no detail.

"I will want to meet the man in question."

Startled, Ijem queried, "Which man, Father?"

"Your husband-to-be!" the Reverend said.

She thought about the possibility. "Father, I am not sure that will be possible."

"Why?"

"I don't know, but it will be difficult. He may not want to come. Besides, he lives in Lagos."

"Is he going to return for Christmas?"

"I think so."

"Okay, find out if he will return, we'll take it from there."

"Yes, Father!"

"I'll want to explain to him the value of education in case he doesn't understand," the Rev. Father explained why he needed to intervene. He paid her, and she left.

Her business continued. Ijem prayed like never before during this period. She wept, promised that she was ready to keep her hair low and vowed never to change her clothes all through her stay in the higher institution if she ever gets into one.

One month later, Ijem fell sick. It was on December 24 of that year. The thoughts of what would transpire between her betrothed husband and the priest kept pushing her blood pressure high. She could not even confide in any family member because that was the last topic they would want to discuss with her.

On the 26th, Jack, her betrothed husband, arrived. Ijem informed the priest and he put a call through to him and fixed an appointment with him at 10:00 am of the 28th.

"Come!" Jack yelled at Ijem. "What did you discuss with one Rev. Fr. Mmaduka that called me this evening?"

With a trembling tone, she mumbled, "Education and employment."

Looking her in the face, with arms akimbo, he queried, "Is it emproyment (employment) before education or education before emproyment? Which is it? Chike Obi! I don't know whether you left your umbilical cord in any higher institution that it has become to you a do-or-die-affair. Must we go over this all the time? How many times have I told you that I don't want this issue *laised* (raised) ever again? You may go to school but only when I can afford it, after having *childlen* (children). Why would you always disturb me with education this, school that? You just go about *compraining* (complaining) to *evely* (every) ear that cares to *risten* (listen). I am into Clearing and Forwarding ... I will make money with time but I'm not going to steal to fund your education. In fact, why does that *pliest* (priest) want to see me? What is my business with any of these? What if I *lefuse* (refuse) to show up for the appointment? This is the last topic I want to discuss. I don't want anybody to spoil my *Chlismass* (Christmas). In fact, I am not going anywhere. *Peliod* (period)!"

"You don't know this priest yet he called you, and made an appointment. You don't even know what he wants to tell you," Ijem calmly said.

"He can keep whatever it is to himself. I don't care!" Jack yelled.

With misty eyes she pleaded, "I think you should just go and see him and hear him out. But if you insist, then call him and cancel the appointment so he doesn't cancel other appointments waiting for you."

"Anyway, I will just go there. But anything he says, I will not commit to anything. Better get *leady* (ready) because he said I should come with you." He stormed out of the room. Ijem had a good cry. Her head pounded three times more. Her temperature was at an all-time-high. She wept and prayed. They arrived the parish house and he offered them food. They ate at the dining as Ijem had not been able to eat anything and so the effect of the drugs made her dizzy. They moved over to the sitting room.

"I am very grateful you responded to my call … I really appreciate that. You are welcome."

"Thank you, Father!"

"Yeah, I met Ijem here a couple of months ago. I discovered that she is a young, industrious, intelligent and well-behaved girl. I had a chat with her and learnt that you have plans to take her as a wife and I decided to see you and talk with you," the priest began.

"I am here now, Father."

"What I want to discuss with you concerns her education. I learnt she just concluded her secondary school and learnt that she performed well in her examinations."

"I am aware of that, Father."

"Good! Now I want you to understand that education is very important especially in this our contemporary society. Let me explain its importance with this simple analogy: a child that completes primary education is like somebody in a room and can see within the confines of the room. A child that completes secondary education is likened to somebody standing on a table in a compound and can only see within the confines of the compound but a child that attains higher education is like somebody standing on the high tower and can see farther in the society and the world. I think Ijem should be encouraged to proceed to the tertiary institution. She possesses the touch. All we need is to give her the battery, and the light will shine for all to see especially when it is dark."

"Father," Jack cleared his throat, meaning to continue, "Father, wait, I understand the importance of education but I cannot afford it now. I never said Ijem will not go to the higher institution but I only said she would do that after giving birth to the *childlen!*"

Rev. Fr. Mmaduka opened his eyes in amazement.

"Ijem, how old are you now?"

"I am going to be seventeen, Father ..."

"Only seventeen, and you are talking about having children? Jack, please this is the best time for her to go to school if you ever want her to. Do you know the responsibility that comes with childbirth and raising of children? This is the only time she can do this. She is still very young. If she gets admission now, in four years, she will be about twenty or twenty-one."

Jack looked the other way, stern and straight-faced. The priest observed him for a while, looked at Ijem and shook his head in disbelief and pity for the young girl. He only imagined how much she must have suffered in her life without even knowing who her biological father was. "Okay!" the Rev. Father continued, "Jack, I am offering to pay her school fees and buy her books while you will take care of her accommodation and feeding. You know, she would need to be fed and live in a house, school or no school." Ijem was startled.

"Rev. Father, you mean you will pay my school fees?" she quickly went on her knees. "Thank you very much, Father. Thank you, God bless you!"

"It's okay, Ijem, please, get up and sit down," the Rev. Father told her. "You don't need to thank me. Just thank God." Jack sat there and said nothing. He neither showed any excitement nor appreciation for what the priest had just said. After a while, the Rev. Father asked Jack, what he thought about the whole idea.

"Father, I am not her *parent* and so I have no say in what you have just suggested. I will convey your offer to her people and whatever they say will be conveyed to you."

"Okay, but since you are trying to take her as a wife, and you said your only predicament was the tuition, that's why I offered to help because I believe it will help her a lot. And for a brilliant young girl ..." he trailed off. Jack kept mute, instead he started hitting the bunch of keys on his laps, shaking his right leg furiously. "Okay, take my message home as you said, I will be expecting your response as soon as possible." On that note, they

130

bid him goodbye and left. They said nothing to each other on their way home. Ijem was only praying in her spirit, thanking God for bringing a genuine help to her.

"This will not happen. I am not going to take this madness. What is wrong with her?" Jack soliloquised. After series of tantrums and annoying venoms in the name of angry words, thrown about by Jack, he dashed out of the compound, exasperated at the development.

"Ijem, you better get married and leave this house. We need space here. We don't have enough rooms to contain us in this house. Just follow your husband," Emeka, Ijem's uncle, fumed. "I will just bury you alive if this man changes his mind because of this your education madness. Call your mother and tell her of the terrible mistake you are about to make in the name of going to school. I don't want to hear that education nonsense in this house, ever again. We don't have money to fund that kind of madness."

"What is so difficult to understand in what Emeka has just said, ehn, Ijem?" Chiazo yelled, adding his own voice to the issue.

In all of this, Ijem had no one on her side. She cried profusely, talking to herself. *Why is my own this difficult? All along, I had believed it was lack of money, but now that a genuine person is willing to help me, ordinary consent has become a problem!* She decided to go and talk with her husband-to-be. She got to his room, entered and knelt down. "Please, I need your support. I need to go to the higher institution. It will be a dream come true. Please, let us accept the offer that the Rev. Father made to pay my tuition, please! I will manage the rest. I won't make my hair. I won't mind cutting my hair just to make sure I don't spend money on frivolous things. I will use only the clothes I already have. Please, just let me go, please. Do not let this opportunity pass me by, please. This is what I have wished for, all my life, please!"

"Ehn eh!" Jack interrupted her, raising his left hand in disagreement. "Just hold it right there. I think it's time you choose between me and this your education. I think you should choose which one is more important to you." Ijem got up in disbelief.

"Are you saying you won't support me on this? That means you never really wanted me to go to school, and you used the lack of funds as your reason. Well, this is a God-given opportunity and I think we should grab it with both hands," Ijem said.

"Take that your so-called offer and tell your kinsmen to return the bride price I paid on your head," he threatened. Ijem watched him with her eyes narrowed, and her teeth clenched, mindful not to say anything further, especially in anger. She shook her head in disbelief, turned and left his house.

It was evening and nobody had entered the kitchen not to talk of having cooked anything in the house. Nnedimma was under another one of her asthmatic attacks! Ijem herself was sick, too, obviously from the raging battle of making her family believe and key into the need for her to go to a higher institution. The atmosphere was dull and all tensed up.

After mulling over the whole situation, Ijem went over to Nnedimma, where she sat on an *okpoga* and confronted her, saying, "Nne, is it that you don't want any of your children to be educated properly?" None of your own children completed secondary school not to talk of getting into a higher institution. All along, the excuse has been that we do not have money. But now that we have a genuine help coming from above, why are you people not accepting the offer? Nne, it's only your 'yes' that the Rev. Fr. Mmaduka needs. He needs only your yes, Mama, and I will be on my way to a tertiary institution," Ijem said with her eyes misting again.

"But Nwam, your husband does not support that we accept that kind of offer coming from another man," Nnedimma said stiffly.

"What man are you talking about? Nne! A priest, a man of God! Nne, I am not living with this man yet, and it's clear he does not want to support me in my dream of going to school. Do you want me to spend my entire life selling recharge cards, oranges or pap in the village market?" Ijem asked her grandmother defiantly.

"*Tufiakwa!* God forbid!" Nnedimma spat out.

"Since you don't want that, I need your support now, Nne. Don't you want your grandchild to work in a bank or a multinational company or live and work abroad so you can visit me? Don't you want to live a better life, enjoy like some other women?" Ijem allowed her grandmother to get the drift.

After a moment Nnedimma said, "Why not, my daughter? I do. In fact, all my suffering will end with you. You are the child specially created to wipe away my tears and calm my spirit especially in my old age as it is at the moment." She brightened up.

Cashing in on her grandmother's mood, Ijem said, "I like the spirit. Nnem, this is the opportunity we have been waiting for. Please, help me. Please, convince them, please, Nne."

"It's okay, my dear, wipe your tears."

Not long after that, Nnedimma summoned all of them to a meeting. It was a family gathering–Emeka, Chiazo and Jack. Ijem was inside the house but not in their midst thinking it best to excuse herself for fear of her presence being a problem. But from where she stood behind the slightly ajar door, she could hear their discussion. "My children, as you can all see, there is no substitute for education for Ijem. I have been with her since she was just a child. She had always wanted this. Now that the opportunity has presented itself, let us give her our support. Nothing else will make her happy if not granting her this request," Nnedimma cajoled. Jack reluctantly accepted. The others nodded their approvals.

Word was sent to Rev. Fr. Mmaduka. He gave her money to get her examination registration done for a polytechnic since that of the university had ended. She eventually got admission to study Banking and Finance at the polytechnic. The course of study really did not matter to her anymore. All she wanted was to attain higher education. Father Mmaduka paid for her tuition, accommodation, books and even gave her feeding money. The sum of money was put in a sealed envelope and delivered by the priest to her in the presence of Nnedimma in her house. Ijem's joy knew no bounds as she matriculated. She studied hard as if her life depended on how long she studied. Soon the first semester results were released and she performed quite impressively. Out of excitement, she sent her results via SMS to Jack and Rev. Fr. Mmaduka. Jack ignored it. Fr. Mmaduka responded with a terse reply: 'I am very proud of you, Ijem. Keep it up. The sky is your starting point. Here is a recharge card from me for this great performance. Cheers!'

She was so happy and proud she impressed the Rev. Father, at least. She called Jack to confirm if he received the text message that she sent to him. He said to her chagrin, "Well, time will tell what is going on between you and that Rev. Father. Keep on deceiving those you can deceive. I just hope he is a good priest?" Ijem could not believe her ears.

She spent the beginning of her stay in the school battling the issue of suspicion and accusation or the other allegations levelled against her by Jack. It was apparent he was insecure and could do nothing but fight Ijem. From one allegation to another. His accusations became a source of distraction to Ijem. She could barely concentrate on her studies.

She travelled home one afternoon after her lectures to see her grandmother. Without wasting any time she launched out, protesting. "Mama, please I am tired of all these accusatory stories. I cannot go on like this. That man is at least twenty-five years older than I am. If for no other reason, he should see me as a daughter. He would complain to you people about all kinds of scenario he dreams up and all kinds of unthinkable stories and you all would leave whatever you are doing to start calling my cell phone in turns. All these are distractions to me. I need to concentrate in school, Mama. I told you people I didn't want to marry this man but you people are still pushing me. Mama, if anything happens to me in that man's house tomorrow, you people will have yourselves to blame. I am going back to school, I just came to plead with you to stop disturbing me over Jack's constant accusations. I am not living with him yet and the situation is like this. When I start living with him, I am sure he won't even let me greet other people. Think about it, Mama, I am going." Ijem returned to school, the constant allegations further widened the gap between her and Jack. The communication died a natural death just in her first year in the polytechnic.

One year later, she finished her Ordinary National Diploma and went to Lagos for her Industrial Training (IT). After a few interviews, she was picked to do her one-year IT at a commercial bank.

135

❧‖ *Twenty* ‖❧

Life as a banker was so beautiful. It gave her a sense of fulfilment. Each time she looked at the mirror and saw how smart and beautiful she looked in her suit and corporate wears, she smiled in appreciation for what Rev. Fr. Mmaduka did and to God who made it possible. Ijem grew more beautiful; her smiles made it glaring, the slight gap in between her upper teeth, even her piercing and seductively attractive eyes became more pronounced. She was loved by her fellow bank staff and she was specially close to the bank manager, Mrs Abong. She had a swell time working at the bank. Some customers appreciated her, leaving her a tip sometimes. She was twenty years old and the youngest staff in the branch; her age earned her some informal duties and the perks that accompanied them; such as sharing and the distribution of birthday cakes, valentine cakes, and so on.

One morning, Ijem noticed a customer waiting to be attended to while she tried logging off the last customer in her system. "Good morning, Sir, and how may I help you?" Upon lifting her face to see who the customer was, it turned out to be Jack, her betrothed husband! Ijem was not really surprised as she already knew that Jack lived somewhere around her office. But to Jack, it was the shock of the millennium. He stood there, wide-eyed, mouth agape, and yet speechless!

"Mr Jack! Surprise! surprise!" she said, smiling. "How is everybody, how are you doing?

Still trying to take in the situation, Jack managed to mutter, "Fine." Ijem paused and stared at her estranged husband-to-be that had gone on a sabbatical for a while and said to him again, "So, how may I help you?"

Sucking in his breath, he said, "I made a payment into someone's account but he complained that it hadn't *leflected* (reflected) in his account.

"May I have the account detail and the deposit slip, the evidence of payment?" He handed her the blue-coloured deposit slip. "Please, sit down over there and give me a few minutes." She went and checked the transaction and saw that it had reflected.

Jack left the bank without saying another word to her, obviously scurrying out of the banking hall in shock. When he had left, Ijem mused, muttering to herself. *What a world!* She smiled mischievously and allowed a thought pass through her mind. *Now I am sure he's seen me and the obvious fact that I'm beginning to see the brighter side of the kind of life that I had told him about. Thank you, Lord. Please, always bless Rev. Fr. Mmaduka for me.*

In less than a week or thereabout, Jack visited the bank three times and always left the premises in the same manner; usually without uttering a word to her. Instead she would be the one trying to start a conversation. The encounter by Ijem's reckoning were all exciting and very pleasant, a kind of Pyrrhic victory! To some extent, she suspected that the man may have deliberately visited the bank the second and the third time just to steal more glances at the still very young, radiant, beautiful and gorgeously dressed damsel that he had abandoned and not seen for so long. After those three occasions, he never communicated with her and neither did Ijem bother to get in touch with him too.

"Hello, Ijem!" greeted a familiar voice on a Friday afternoon. Ijem looked up from her cubicle to behold the ever charming young man whom she had always admired for his eloquence, smart sense of dressing, confidence and carriage. He was one of the bank's customers who had been to the branch a few times since Ijem started working there.

"Good afternoon, Sir!" she politely greeted. "I hope your weekend is splendid?" Ijem teased.

"I am sure I can say so if only you'll accept to go to dinner with me after work today?" he said, smiling and looking up to her for a favourable response.

"I'll rather go home and rest. You already know about the usual traffic. It's always very hectic. I stay in Surulere, and the traffic from Victoria Island can be very exhausting. I don't see how I can cope, adding that to a dinner," she lamented.

"Yeah, I understand, even though I don't live in Lagos. I just visit for official assignments. But I will drop you off after that and that would be when the traffic would have subsided, if you don't mind? Please?" he pleaded.

"Okay then, other customers are waiting," she whispered and politely discharged him.

"Catch ya later then," he winked at her and left.

✳   ✳   ✳   ✳   ✳

At about thirty minutes past 5 o' clock in the evening, the dashing young man returned to the bank but was asked by security staff to wait. He went back to the car park and waited in his car, listening to some music. After some time she emerged from the bank carrying her handbag. He saw her and quickly stepped out of the car, gave her a hug and opened the car for her to get in. They drove to a restaurant, ordered some drinks and food.

The drinks were served first; they sipped and talked about

their offices and work. Soon, the food arrived and they ate in silence for a while. Then, he cleared his throat. "I'll like to know you more than just your name, if you don't mind," he said tentatively.

"Well, I haven't got much to tell you. I am Ijem Obidi, from Afanasaa town in the south-eastern part of Nigeria. I am a student on industrial training, and at the moment on attachment with the bank. That's all," Ijem said as she fiddled with the straw in her glass of juice.

"Okay, that is interesting! At least now, I know you're not a spirit because you have told me your place of origin," he joked as they smiled at each other.

Ijem looked away shyly as would any girl who is a little bit awestruck by the opposite sex whom she admires. She then summoned up courage to ask him, "Will you please reciprocate and tell me about yourself?"

"Of course! Without you asking. I had wanted you to shoot first. Anyway, my name is Ade. I am from Umudike in the south-eastern part of the country. I am a medical doctor. I studied Medicine, first degree here in Nigeria, but I will be travelling out next week. Wednesday to be precise, to the Johns Hopkins Medical College in the United States for my post-graduate studies," he said.

"*Waoh*! That's wonderful," she screamed. "Are you serious?"

"Yes, I am."

"I am so happy for you, Ade. This is great. But how come you bear the name Ade since you said you are from the south-east?"

"You see, my mother is from the west but got married to my father who is from the east. It was my mum who gave me that name. Of course, I do have an Igbo name, Ikem," he explained.

"Okay, I see!" With that, they exchanged phone numbers.

"Soon, this number won't be relevant but when I get to the US I will call to let you have my international line ..." Ijem became transfixed ... She was apparently hanging on every word that Ade spoke. She began to fantasise and started appreciating the many attributes of her newfound friend, Ade. They ended up having a long chat, talking about nothing in particular. Later, he dropped her off when the traffic had eased off.

"Thank you so very much," she said.

"No, I'm supposed to be the one saying a big thanks. And it's really been nice having this outing with you, Ijem! Thanks for granting me this opportunity. I can say my day has been splendid," he said, smiling. "Hey, can we do this again tomorrow?" he asked, fixing his gaze on her beautiful face. "At least, you won't look official tomorrow!" Ijem was mute. Instead she thought, *Why does he want us to do this again? He will soon leave for the United States. I don't want to start what cannot be sustained.* Breaking her thought, he said, "Please, Ijem," he pleaded, grabbing her palms in his, "let's meet tomorrow. It's a Saturday, I am sure you won't be working tomorrow," he said breathlessly.

Reluctantly, Ijem said, "Okay! Ade, let's see how tomorrow will be."

"I take that to be a yes," he teased.

"You know better."

"Yeah, I sure do."

"Okay then, have a good night," she said, as she opened the door to leave the car.

"No, no, not so fast, Ijem!" He drew her closer, turned on the car's roof light, stared into her face, and said, "How I wish I had met you earlier than now," as he squeezed and rubbed her arms. She deeply felt the same way but managed to conceal the feeling. He pleaded again, "Please, let's see tomorrow. Take care of you and sleep like we had a special day." He kissed the back of her palm gently. She stepped out of the car and waved him good night as he drove off.

She quite relished the gesture of his kissing the back of her hand. They had great moments of laughter every evening within the few days he had left, before he travelled out for his studies abroad. They went to the beach, the cinemas and a few other open places of recreation. This left lasting impressions in their hearts. They knew that they will miss each other when they eventually parted.

Few days later, Ijem's handbag was snatched by a man on a moving bike on her way home from work. She lost her cell phone and other valuables inside her bag. She regretted having not put down his phone number elsewhere. It was clear to her that Ade would not be able to contact her again. Every now and then she would lapse into a reverie, savouring the memories of the fleeting romance.

As was the policy in the bank, the IT staff who were on attachment, were equally given a target to get new accounts to the bank with a minimum of one million naira deposit. Ijem did all she could, talking to the customers whom she regularly attended to; trying to convince those who did not have an account with her bank to open one. She talked to one of the customers, a certain Dr Ene, who showed interest and promised to give it some thoughts. But even before agreeing to give her proposition a chance he had argued and slugged it out with her.

"Why should I open an account with your bank? I already have several accounts in five other banks."

"Sir, I am sure you know those are current accounts, and they charge you enormous commission on transfer (COT)?"

"Yes! That's normal."

"Sir, my bank is offering you an account that you'll operate with a cheque book but no COT will be charged."

"Are you serious?"

"Yes, Sir, which is the real reason why you should have an account with our bank," she smiled, knowing that he was going to do something regarding her proposal.

"Okay, I'll think about it."

"I will be expecting your positive response, Sir," she said.

Some days later, Dr Ene called and asked her to deliver an account opening package to his office; which she did. Surprisingly, he opened an account with ten million naira lodged in it.

One of those days, Ijem had a sad experience at the bank. She could not balance her ledger at the end of the day. She had a shortage of a hundred thousand naira. Usually, the bank would not close until they resolved the problem. Everybody was unhappy staying at the office till 11 pm. She wept so bitterly because the only option would be to debit her account, and credit the bank with the shortfall. But that would entail working for four months without pay if that happened. At 11:35 pm, the head office of the bank granted a permission for their branch to close for the day on the condition that they would rectify the problem first thing the next business day.

Ijem cried so hard that she became absent-minded most of the time at the bank.

In her calculation, she had hoped that after working in the bank during the period of her attachment, she would have saved some money for her mother to start her own business. Then she also had hoped she would keep the rest for her school, and other things that may require financial attention. But this dream was about to crash.

At the moment, she was hungry as she had only eaten some pieces of biscuit in the morning, and had hoped to get some food after balancing the ledger at the close of business.

When she could not get her books balanced, the hunger fled.

One of her colleagues offered to drop her off at her street as it would have been difficult to get a vehicle to her place at that time of the night. She got into her compound at 12:05 am.

"Why are you coming back so late? You scared me. Try and inform me whenever you are staying out this late. Else I won't open this gate," her landlady snapped without looking at Ijem's direction.

Ijem did not utter a word, instead she dumped herself on her bed and wept silently. Shortly after she had cried for some time, her phone rang. Picking it up, it was Segun, one of her colleagues at the bank. "Hello, girl, I'm sorry, we discovered the excess cash deposited into our company's account contrary to our records. We have a hundred thousand naira."

"Are you serious?"

"Yes."

"Thank God!"

"You are welcome. We actually discovered it earlier even before your boss called for verification. Don't worry, I will bring the teller tomorrow for amendment."

"Thank you, I am very grateful. You just revived me."

"Sorry it took this long, girl. I can only imagine what you were going through. That's why I couldn't sleep knowing you may not be fine." He now launched into another business ... "You know I like you a lot. Just that you are taking your time, and it's possible that you may be checking me out."

"Go *jo!*" Ijem said breaking out with smiles even as tears were still streaming down her cheeks. Tears of sorrow turning into tears of joy.

"I will see you in the morning. Good night, girl!"

"Good night!" Ijem said too. Immediately, she started calling her other colleagues and contacted her boss.

She got registered for Direct Entry into the University of Ibadan to study Accounting. One of the requirements for the registration was her OND result and a transcript. She needed time off work to travel to the school where she did her OND.

"Excuse me, Ma," she said standing before the branch's operation manager. The woman in dealing with her previously had been mean. She came hoping that this very mean woman that had just been transferred recently to the branch from somewhere she did not bother to check, would not be mean by refusing to grant her request.

"Yes, what's it, Ijem?"

"Ma, please, I need to take some days off to travel to my school and collect my result and transcript because I want to apply for Direct Entry and the registration has already commenced."

"Sorry, there is no room for such luxury for anybody now in the bank. We are short of personnel. Just go back to your duty post and don't disturb my peace," the manager said dismissively.

"Ma, please."

"Excuse me, Ijem. As you can see, I am busy," she snapped at her. Ijem returned to her cubicle and continued working.

The next day, at the close of business hours, when she was distributing cake from one of the staff of the bank who was celebrating her birthday, she got into the bank's head office to deliver her share of the cake.

"Good evening, Ma!"

"How are you, Ijem?"

"I am fine, Ma."

"But your face doesn't look it." Ijem held out the tray containing the cake in her two hands, fixed her gaze at the entrance door to avoid making eye contact with Mrs Abong. Madam Abong was an Efik woman, very strict when it came to work ethics, and getting results. She was dreaded by every other staff of the branch, but she took a special liking for Ijem. She made a point of always asking about her wellbeing, and that of her family. She had often offered her helping tips and encouraged her and tried so often to make her feel at ease around her. Ijem was well aware of that, and was determined not to take undue advantage of that. But having found herself in a tight corner, she decided to latch unto that knowledge and call in the favour!

"My dear, talk to me, I know you too well to know that something is wrong. What is it?"

"Ma, remember I told you I wanted to apply for a direct entry admission into a university?"

"Yes."

"Now, the registration has started and I need to go and get my result from the school so as to enable me apply."

"So, what is the problem with that?"

"Madam Tola won't grant me some days off!"

"I see, is that all?"

"Yes, Ma."

"Okay then, you don't need to worry," she nodded. "I will handle it. Go and write your application, and take it to Tola. I will talk to her now."

"Yes, Ma," she said with a shy smile. Mrs Abong immediately dialed the intercom and spoke into it.

"You can go now, she will endorse your letter for my approval. But I am leaving the office now. So once you get her recommendation, don't bother about my approval, you already have it, so you can travel tomorrow."

"Thank you very much, Ma. God bless you. I am very grateful."

❧ *Twenty-one* ☙

Ijem travelled and arrived at her grandmother's place in the evening of the next day being a Wednesday. On Thursday, she got set and went to her school. She regretted making that trip. The result was not ready. In fact, they were yet to start computing the results from different lecturers. She felt so bad for two things; she would have to take permission from the office again and she would have to spend another round of transport fare. The deep feeling of frustration made her almost cry. After hanging around the school premises for a while and ensuring she had exhausted all possible channels to see if she could get the transcript, she left for her mother's place, at Ikenga.

Her mother had relocated to Ikenga since she was separated from Enuma by the welfare department. She had been living there long before Ijem got admission into the polytechnic. Another surprise awaited her as she arrived at the house and met no one. The compound was quiet and lonely with overgrown weeds competing for space. She sat on a low guava tree branch in the compound. She was just looking round the compound, wondering where her mother could be. Nneka had no phone. She waited until a man sauntered into the compound. She recognised him as a co-tenant of her mother's. "Good afternoon, Sir. Please, I am looking for my mother, Mrs Nneka Enuma."

"I am not too sure about her whereabouts, but I know she

went to the hospital two days ago."

"Seriously? Which hospital, please?" Ijem queried.

"The only hospital here. It's that private one down the road."

Just then Anene came in. She rushed to hug him and asked him almost immediately, "Nna, where is Mum?"

"Hospital!" the little boy said tersely.

"What is wrong with her? Which hospital? Anyway let's go, let's go!" Anene quickly picked up the spare clothes he had come to grab and they left, striding to the hospital. The little boy ran after her all the way to the hospital due to Ijem's anxiety and long strides in her bid to get to the hospital quickly.

Entering the hospital, Ijem noticed a nurse sitting at her work station, and quickly went over to her. "Good evening. Please, where is my mother? What is wrong with her?" she blurted out without wasting time for pleasantries. After ascertaining who she was, and establishing the relationship between her and the patient, she was taken to see the doctor first.

When she was ushered in to see the doctor, he barely looked up from his file as he talked to the visitor in a nonchalant manner that some doctors had adopted in treating patients, and their relations. The attitude was said to have crept into some hospitals because of experiences that doctors had had in the past; when patients ended up being unable to pay for drugs, treatments and services rendered.

"Your mother needs at least two pints of blood. Unfortunately, we can't do anything as the hospital policy requires that a deposit be made before the commencement of treatment. You know that the blood she requires comes from a blood bank. We really need money to do all those," the doctor explained. Nneka had lapsed into unconsciousness and so could not rally around for the money herself, and Anene was too young to do anything.

"Jeez!" Ijem exclaimed. "So you would have watched my mother die, Doctor? Just because you needed a deposit? How could she have gotten the money for you when she is unconscious? Well, I just hope she is still stable. I just hope you people have not hurt my mother. Get the blood and start treating her immediately," she prattled, while the doctor sat back in his chair and watched. She paid for the deposit.

She sat beside her mother lost in thoughts: *these doctors are so wicked! So if I hadn't come here now it would have become another story. Maybe this was the real reason why I returned home when the result for which I had travelled was not ready. Hmm! As they say, every disappointment is really a blessing in disguise. Thank God I came just in time to help.*

Two days later, Nneka was discharged and Ijem was happy to have returned home to come rescue her mother. She returned to Lagos and was granted permission to pick up her result one month later. She did her registration.

She concluded her one year attachment in the bank and got admission into a university to study Accounting. She gave her mother some money from her savings to change her line of business since her regular sickness was attributed to the heat from the fire and the smoke that spewed from the kitchen. She was indeed engaged in the running of a *buka* business.

Nneka had been separated from Enuma for many years by the welfare officials who had advised her to stay away from her spouse, preferably anywhere she considered safe. She was also advised to carry out any business of her choice. She chose to continue doing her cooking business. She had started the cooking business when Enuma, her spouse, forbade her travelling out to Ogbaru to buy yams. He had believed that travelling would afford her the opportunity to tango with lorry drivers and other men. She had started by cooking large portions on the market day which held every four days. She would wake up at 12:30 am and start preparing the food. At 5:30 am, she would have been done. She would pack the big warmers containing the rice, *ofe-akwu*, beans, yam, plates and spoons and a gallon of water on a wheel barrow and head out to the marketplace.

Sometimes, she would place flat woods on the wheel barrow to create additional space. She would push the wheel barrow in the dark, and through rough paths to the bus stop where she would now set up and sell.

The business was doing well, if not for any other reason but to enable her feed her children. She was busy in a productive way. But at times she became regularly ill and the doctor attributed the cause to the nature of her business—the fire. Now, it was time to give up the business since the sickness was becoming too frequent. Nneka used the money that Ijem gave to her to start selling foodstuff such as crayfish, palm oil, vegetable oil and other condiments.

❧ Twenty-two ❧

After her matriculation, Ijem got settled at the University of Ibadan. It was a different environment compared to her former school. They were now one hundred and fifty in a class compared to the five hundred students in her former school. She lived in the school hostel now but lived off campus in her former school due to lack of school accommodation. The university she attended was far away from home, in another state but the polytechnic was in her state of origin. From the savings she made, she was able to pay her tuition, her accommodation and other freshmen fees. Rev. Fr. Mmaduka was happy when he received the news of her admission but said he was no longer in a position to help her.

Rev. Fr. Mmaduka had been transferred to a very local and small outstation church which had just been converted into a new parish of the Catholic Church. He could barely feed himself. When Ijem saw him, he looked quite lean and shabby. He was just managing to survive on the work he was doing for God.

Meanwhile, Ijem survived on local delicacies such as *ewedu* and *amala, ewa agoyin* and *Agege* bread which were cheap compared to other foods available on campus.

Her first year was rough but it went well. When the results were published Ijem made good grades. After the second semester examinations, there was a three months break. Ijem travelled to Lagos in search of a vacation job.

She went to stay with one of her cousins, Kene, who lived in the Ejigbo area of Lagos. Kene was not doing well in his business. He was seriously contemplating relocating to the village. He lived in the slums of Ejigbo. There was no road to the uncompleted bungalow where he lived. Only a footpath led to his house. The house was close to a big canal. There was no electricity in the house, and Kene could not afford a generator. The house was uncompleted because they said the owner had an undefined problem bordering on mental instability or something along that line. The house was just roofed, and Kene managed to plaster his room and put a ceiling. They usually bought water from a borehole in the neighbourhood. It was like back to square one for Ijem. An almanac of a company which hung on the wall was the only decor in the house. She wished she could get a better place which would actually give her a feeling that she was in Lagos. But that was not the case. She really didn't have a choice. What mattered was to get the vacation job that would enable her rack up her savings for school.

She got a vacation job in Ikoyi in a private firm. It was quite a distance going to work in Ikoyi from Ejigbo. She spent so much on transportation but she still managed to save. One fateful day, she ran into Dr Ene, yet again, after several months of her dealing with him as a customer in the bank she worked in. To her surprise, he was the manager of the company.

As if to compensate for the account he had opened with her when she did her attachment with the bank, he started making sexual advances towards her. It was serious. He did not relent in making her uncomfortable with his sexual advances.

"Just be my girlfriend, and I will change your life forever. I will rent you a big flat in school and furnish it. I will make you one of the big girls on campus. Just say yes to me. I have all it takes to make you happy and comfortable," he went on and on.

"I am sorry, Sir, I can't date you. You are my boss. What should

I be doing with you? Please, I will really appreciate it if we drop this topic," she pleaded with him.

✲   ✲   ✲   ✲   ✲

One day he came into the office and having heard Ijem talking with another junior staff how she desired to have a laptop because they had wireless network in their university, Dr Ene called her the next morning into his office. "Ijem, my dear, I learnt you needed a laptop. I have got one for you to show you how much I love you and how willing I am to make you live like a princess, that you are. Here is the laptop for you," he said, pointing at the carton of a branded laptop on his desk. Ijem could not get hold of herself; she was swept off her feet by that seemingly thoughtful gesture of his. She thanked him so much and tried getting hold of the laptop. Just then Dr Ene said to her, "Not-so-fast, my dear girl, this laptop is yours but you will take it only on one condition. Just be mine ..."

Ijem gently removed her hands from the laptop, and said with misty eyes, "Sir, I really need this laptop and I know you can afford to give me one. God will bless you if you can leave it for me without any condition." Dr Ene maintained his stance. Ijem left his office frustrated.

Ijem had a special liking for Dr Ene despite his misbehaviour but Dr Ene could not stand the embarrassment and terminated her vacation job, one month earlier than planned.

Soon, it was three months and the school reopened. Ijem had managed to save just enough to cater for her school fees but not enough to take care of her daily needs and accommodation. She decided to squat with one of her friends who lived in the school hostel. Things became tougher as the semester went by.

✲   ✲   ✲   ✲   ✲

What am I supposed to do? Who will I talk to at this stage? I need to finish school but I cannot afford it. If I quit at this stage, all these years would be wasted, all the money spent so far. She battled with her thoughts and the fear of dropping out of school. *Maybe I should ask for a deferral from the school authority so that I can work for one year and raise my school fees.*

She managed through thick and thin till the end of the first semester of her second year in school. At the end of the first semester, she wrote a letter for deferment. She went to the registrar's office to submit her letter only to be told, "Sorry, the person in charge of that is not available. He would return next week. So check back next week." She walked out of the administrative building of the university.

Two days later, it was announced that the Academic Staff Union of Universities (ASUU) had embarked on an indefinite strike. All students left the campus and travelled to their homes. Ijem again returned to Lagos, and to Kene's house. She discovered that her cousin, Kene, had changed his line of business. He was now hawking small items such as brushes, combs, key holders, cotton buds and so on, all displayed in a wheelbarrow. He could no longer afford to pay the rent for his shop. Ijem faced yet another hard time trying to feed herself and her cousin. She was lucky to land a job at a firm with her OND result for the four months the strike lasted. She then decided not to defer her studies any longer.

She thought and imagined, peradventure such a strike happened again, what was she going to do with herself? After dwelling so much on the thoughts, she decided to settle with a business as a retailer in school. She was then faced with making a choice of business. *Maybe I should start the kind of business I was doing before—selling of recharge cards? At least, that will be manageable given that I live in the school hostel, in a room populated with four students. I don't have much space. I have just my wardrobe. But again this recharge card business does not yield much profit these*

days because so many people are now into the business. In fact, it is no longer lucrative. What else can I possibly do? I know items students can use will definitely sell. Yes, all those people that display goods in the hostel. Hmm, I think I now have a better idea. She settled with the idea.

She took fifty thousand naira out of her savings and went to Idumota market with no definite goods or items in mind. "How do you sell your panties? I mean on wholesale?"

"Madam, we only do wholesale. The price depends on the type you want. They are not the same price. We have those that go for seven hundred, eight hundred, nine hundred and one thousand two hundred naira. So, it's your choice."

Ijem bought dozens of panties; different colours, designs and styles. She also bought packets of handkerchiefs, leggings, panty hoses, make-up items such as lipsticks, eye shadows, mascara, blushes, foundation and so on, even though she did not make use of any of those things. She bought earrings and other jewelries that she believed could sell in the school environment. This shopping took her three days after which she arranged all her goods in three big *Ghana Must Go* bags and returned to school.

Back in school and set for the second semester, business kicked off. She put up posters in all the female hostels listing out her goods, her address and contact number. She also made handbills which she distributed as she went around the campus. Business was doing fine. She would display her goods at the hostel lobby. She got calls always from students requesting for one good or the other with their specifications. She would call her customers to send down goods to her from Lagos. Sometimes, she would go and buy the goods herself. It was hectic, stressful but she was happy, she was making good profit. One evening after selling wares to some students who came to her room to buy stuff, her bed was littered with things to be packed. Her roommate, Joan, said with irritation, "Why are you even stressing yourself carrying bags of *Ghana Must Go* about in the name of selling to make money? There are better ways to make money. I just hate how you are stressing yourself and disturbing our peace in this room. Must you do business to pay your fees? Must you? Of course not." She went closer and held her shoulders, "Ijem, you are a very fine girl. Many guys out there just to have a taste of your soft body will date you. You don't know the value of what you have. Can't you see me? Check me out now. Don't I eat well? Dress well? Live well and above all have enough cash to settle just anything? See all the time you just wasted with those girls just for a paltry sum of one thousand naira. How much is your gain out of that amount? Ijem, this is not worth it, trust me. You are simply suffering yourself!"

"So, Joan, what do you expect me to do now? How do I cope with paying my school fees and taking care of myself?"

Smiling, she said, "Eh-he, now you are talking! Don't worry. I will gladly hook you up. I will hand you over to a man that will take very good care of you..."

"Well, Joan, thank you. I don't wish to be handed over to any man. I have many of them disturbing me wherever I go. I am almost done with my studies and so I don't see the need of any of those," Ijem said.

"Hmm, look at this girl. You are almost done with what? Girl, wake up. This is just your second year, second year not your final year. Just think about it and tell me when you are ready. I just think it's an opportunity to grab instead of playing *Santa Nwegbe* and earning yourself the epithet, *Miss Black handbag*! Step up, Girl. I am ashamed that I have you as my roommate."

"Na wao! I don't see why you should be taking analgesic for my headache. Please, don't compound my problems. Just pretend that I am not here with you as a roommate since you are ashamed of me!"

✻   ✻   ✻   ✻   ✻

Ijem travelled home on a weekend to see her grandmother. She met with her maternal uncle, Patty, and explained her plight. He promised to support her in his own little way. He would call her daily to encourage her. He supported her with words of advice. Sometimes, he would send her some money. She was happy. She was grateful she had him. "You are my true friend and uncle. You show me so much care and love that I just feel I have a father in you. Can I call you Daddy, please? That is how you make me feel, like you are my daddy. Your kind words spur me on to action. You listen to me and talk to my soul. You are there for me when I think I am alone. God bless you for me."

From that day, she had the pleasure of addressing Uncle Patty as 'Daddy'.

Towards the end of the second semester of her second year at the university, some of her friends and course mates urged her to contest for a political position in her department.

"I don't have money to waste, please!" was her response.

"There is nothing like wasting money, Ijem. I just think you can do it and you have all it takes to be an executive of your department. The positions available for second year students include: Public Relations Officer, Financial Secretary, Treasurer and Assistant Secretary. Which one of these do you think you can go for?"

"I don't know, please. Just let me be. I am too busy to join school politics," she retorted defiantly.

"I just think you should try. It will be challenging but interesting. I would have contested but my CGPA is below the benchmark," Ada said regretfully.

Ijem later picked the form for the post of Treasurer for five hundred naira. She got a female lecturer, Dr Mrs Akinola, to endorse her application.

"I am only going to endorse this because I am impressed by your academic performance so far. Your cumulative grade point average is impressive. But I am worried."

"About what, Ma?"

"That you are going to be distracted by this politics. I will only sign this on the condition that you promise me that you will maintain this CGPA."

"I cross my heart, Ma. It won't go down. I will always give my best."

"I hope so, you know when you students get into politics, you forget your mission here at first and start chasing winds."

"No, Ma, it won't be like that," Ijem assured her.

"I am only taking you by your words, and that is why I am signing this. Good luck."

"Thank you very much, Ma."

Dr Akinola endorsed her form. She organised and did her campaign. On the day of manifesto, she swept many people off their feet by her delivery. After the election, she won the post of the Treasurer of her department. The newly elected executives were inaugurated shortly before the school shut down for a one month vacation.

❧|| *Twenty-three* ||❧

The school reopened a month later and ushered Ijem into her third year in the university; She was able to eke out her school fees from her business proceeds. She was fulfilled and happy. She was gradually approaching the finishing line. The help she got from Uncle Patty was channeled to helping her grandmother and her step-siblings. Throughout her stay in the school, she would usually travel home at intervals to see her grandmother. On each of these visits, she would spend the money she had at hand on food and drugs for her grandmother. She hated to see her still suffering and sick after very many years of anguish and abject poverty. She wished she could perform some magic and change things for her beloved grandmother. Out of pity, Ijem would always just manage to spare her transport fare back to school. Unlike other students who got replenished and restocked with pocket money, provisions and foodstuff when they travelled home, Ijem would instead take home provisions, foodstuff and money to her grandmother.

She continued her business without shame or discontent. It was quite tedious having to run her business, attend classes, attend executive meetings and also study. Anyway, she always tried to squeeze out time to read her books. She would usually go to the library to avoid the customers that would always come to buy one thing or the other at just anytime they pleased.

Some would have her empty the contents of the bags on her bed without buying anything on grounds that they could not see what they wanted to buy, the colour or design they wanted. It was such a task having to do that many times in a day.

Towards the middle of the first semester of her 300 level, the executive members agreed that the students of the department would embark on an excursion trip to the Federal Capital Territory. The president of the departmental student union government was advised to take a trip to Abuja in the company of another member of the executive, to do the necessary arrangements for all the places they would visit and the accommodation. Later on the next day, he met with Ijem in front of the department. "Ijem, I have been looking for you. I heard you were having a class so I decided to wait."

"I hope all is well?"

"Yes, all is well. I just want to talk with you concerning the upcoming trip to Abuja."

"What about it?" Ijem asked. They walked and sat on the rail in front of the department's building.

"I need to make this trip with someone but I don't want to go with Kachi. He has been disturbing me about it. I think it's wise to go with a female member of the executive instead of another male. You know what I mean. It will balance our representation. The school is not for males alone, we should have females. I will appreciate it if you can do the trip to Abuja with me," he said.

"Why me?"

"I know you have been to Abuja before and this will help. Besides, Modesta, the vice-president, said she will be seeing her project supervisor next week and so would not be available to go with me," he revealed.

"See, Presido, I will miss classes especially those of Prof. Bode who does not give notes or handout. If I am not in the class, it will be difficult for me to get the topic he would treat next."

"That will not be a problem at all. We will go and explain to him. After all he is the head of department and he is aware of this journey. He would even give us a letter of introduction."

"Okay, if that is the case, I will go with you, Mr President," she said laughing.

"Thank you, Madam Treasurer, We will leave on Sunday."

"Okay, but where are we going to stay? Do you know anybody in Abuja?"

"No, I grew up in Onitsha, I have never even been anywhere close to Abuja before," he said. *This is serious!* she thought.

She exhaled while tapping on the books she was carrying on her left hand. "I have been to Abuja twice. The first was when I was in my former school when the Nigerian Federation of Catholic Students did a convention in Abuja. I was so eager to see Abuja and so I went and it was very interesting. Apart from the programme, we visited places like the Millennium Park, Transcorp Hilton, Silverbird Cinemas. We saw the headquarters of Central Bank of Nigeria (CBN)," she narrated. Mr President was lost, only hanging on every word she spoke. He was mentally capturing the seemingly scenic city of Abuja. Ijem continued, "The second time was during the last holidays. I went on an errand for my uncle. I stayed at a friend's place. Someone I knew from Lagos. So maybe I should call him and see if he can accommodate us but he lives in just one room," she warned.

"Okay, please talk to him first and let me know the outcome by tomorrow being Friday."

"All right then, let me run."

Very early on Sunday morning, they met at the park and got their bus tickets to Abuja. It was an interesting trip and particularly exciting for the president since that was his first

Abuja experience. They chatted along on diverse issues, some about their department, their lecturers, the road, the driver, the reason for the trip and so on.

When they arrived Lokoja, the driver drove into a gas station, commonly known as filling station and parked. The passengers thought he wanted to refill his tank not until they had spent about fifty minutes without seeing the driver. Then they all started asking questions. When they found the driver, he arrogantly said that the bus had developed a fault and he thinks they can no longer continue the journey. "The steering is not good. It can pack up anytime," the driver said defiantly. The furious passengers were mad at his impunity. They demanded for refunds. The driver let out a little laugh. "I don't have any money here, you people paid them at the park. They only gave me money for petrol," he said with a straight face. When they had spent the next one and a half hours arguing, ranting and threatening the driver, the passengers, one after the other, made alternative arrangements and resorted to taking other vehicles from Lokoja to Abuja. To Ijem and Presido, it was an additional cost which could raise eyebrows when they would be rendering their account for their trip to Abuja.

They spent four days making all the plans, visiting all the potential places for the excursion.

Meanwhile, the news making the rounds in the department was that the president and Ijem went to Abuja to squander the student associations' funds. In fact, the matter was reported to the Head of Department (HOD). The executive members of the students' association were all summoned to a meeting with the HOD, the students' staff adviser and one additional lecturer who was a priest. Ijem's heart was beating very fast. She felt she should not have gone to Abuja with the president. At the meeting, the HOD introduced the agenda which was the constant complaints about the administration's mode of operation and the recent Abuja trip. The main complainant happened to be Modesta, the vice-president.

She had been a spoiler since her boyfriend failed to contest for the presidency. He was disqualified because his CGPA was below the benchmark. "Sir, since the inception of this administration, things have not been going properly as it's supposed to. I am the vice-president of the association and as such, I think I should be carried along in everything that concerns the association," she started. The HOD and the other lecturers nodded in agreement. "But that is not the case ... Ijem here, the treasurer, has been tagged the madam of the association..." all eyes followed her hand to Ijem who fixed her gaze somewhere else in the HOD's office. In her mind, she thought, *hmm, it looks like I am the bone of contention in this meeting. Hmm, God please. I don't want trouble at all. This was the reason I didn't want to contest at first.* "She is literally in charge of the association's affairs ..." Modesta spat out. Ijem grimaced, and turned sharply to her direction wondering what that statement from the VP could mean.

"Sir, all the projects we have executed so far were all handled by Ijem. She is in charge of the treasury and when she handles projects herself, you all know the implication ..." she said cynically as she rolled her eyes at Ijem. "Just last week again, she only returned from a one-week all-expense paid trip to Abuja with the president. Why should she be the one to travel to Abuja with the president? Why should she even go to Abuja at all? Was it necessary? There was obviously no check on their expenditure," Modesta submitted. Meanwhile Ijem had been raising her hand in objection to what she had been alleged of but was not acknowledged. "This is a serious case!" Modesta said, taking her seat.

Turning his gaze to Ijem, the HOD said, "Ijem, you heard all the allegations that have been levelled against you ..." Ijem nodded. "What do you have to say?" She adjusted her sitting position and sat upright.

"Thank you very much, Sir, for granting me the audience and opportunity to speak. Honestly, I must say that I am surprised at all that the VP just enumerated against me. But they are obvious misconceptions I believe. First, this administration was inaugurated at the end of last semester. School resumed four weeks ago and so we have really not embarked on any major project yet. We don't have much money in the account since most students are yet to pay their departmental dues. The things we have done so far are the things we deemed absolutely necessary. We hired cleaners to clean up the department and that was handled by the financial secretary and the president. We also procured waste bins for the department. That again was done by the assistant secretary. We purchased packets of white board markers for the classes, which was handled by the secretary. The PRO is following up on the stickers and the ID cards for the new students. As you all can see, I did not partake in the execution of any of the mentioned projects. So, I don't understand how it turned out that the VP is accusing me of being in charge of all the projects ..." she trailed off.

"Secondly, she talked about not carrying her along. I am only the treasurer and so it is not my duty to inform her of meetings, or the outcome of meetings except if she asks me and politely too. I only noticed she has always turned up for meetings few minutes to the end of the meeting, and we couldn't possibly start over the meetings to carry her along. I believe she could always liaise with the president or PRO or secretary to bring her up-to-date.

"Thirdly, it is crystal clear that she has a problem with my trip to Abuja with the President. Let me state clearly that I did not lobby to accompany him to Abuja instead he demanded officially and after due considerations, I gave my consent. I missed my lectures while I was away. I am yet to make up for my absence." She shifted her attention to the HOD. "For example, Prof., I missed your classes and I don't know how to get the note yet, and I don't have the textbook either." The HOD smiled. She continued, "Again, we went to Abuja on behalf of the department and it is ideal for the department to cater for our feeding, transportation, accommodation and in some cases, allowances as the VP insinuated, it was supposed to be 'an all-expense paid trip'." She raised her shoulder, spread her hands apart, looking around as if she expected answers from them.

As if on cue, those in attendance started to chip in. "That's right," said the lecturers and the HOD.

"That is true," said the priest.

She continued, "We all know or can imagine the cost of an average hotel room in Abuja for a night. That is what we saved the department for four good days. We went to inconvenience my friend who lives in Abuja. We were supposed to eat good meals, but to save cost, we ate akara and bread all morning. We did 1-0-1, that is, we ate in the morning and night only, throughout the four days. We even walked to some places in a bid to save cost. See now, I have blisters on my foot and so, cannot wear shoes till it heals. What hurts me now is that instead of getting thanks for saving funds for the department, I am being criticised by the VP and her friends, just to tarnish my image," she paused.

"Finally, this trip to Abuja was not my first time to Abuja. So it was not as if I went sight-seeing. In fact, I didn't notice any change since my last visit to Abuja." The lecturers started laughing in admiration of her orderly and captivating speech. "So, I don't see how any of these summed up to 'being in charge of the department's affairs'. I just don't know why some people choose to globalise their personal problems."

"Hahaha!" the gathering burst out, some of the students and the lecturers had a good laugh.

"This girl is really crazy," the priest said pointing at Ijem amidst tearful laughter. Ijem was satisfied. She was happy. At the end, the case was concluded in her favour and the HOD gave her his textbook to read to make up for the classes she missed. She was happy, she bragged about it as they left the HOD's office. "They thought I would be hanged on the cross. Shame!" she mocked when the VP walked past her in obvious exasperation. "Well, I have developed a thick skin for any form of vituperation anybody will try with me," she said happily as she ran down the stairs with the president and the PRO.

✲ ✲ ✲ ✲ ✲

Two months later, Ijem and the president led fifty-five students on an academic tour to the Federal Capital Territory of Nigeria. The trip was exciting, thrilling, fulfilling, fully event packed. It lasted for one week and they lodged at a guest house in the heart of Abuja city. There were side attractions such as going to the cinemas which was a first cinematic experience for most of the participants. Many loved the whole package. But a few were envious of Ijem because she was particularly acknowledged at all the corporate offices they visited. A director at one of the organisations they visited said, "I am happy this is happening so I can rest. Ijem won't take a no for an answer. I told the president that we could not afford to host you now. He accepted but I was surprised Ijem called me and pleaded until I carved out this time. She told me, 'Sir, even if it is for five minutes, we would really appreciate it. We are already looking forward to visiting your organisation. Please, don't cut our dreams short, please!' Those gentle words of hers penetrated my spirit and left me no choice than to create time, despite the tight schedule we run here." He paused, looked around the audience and returned his gaze to Ijem, I just met her, but I think she is a great girl filled with an indomitable doggedness to achieve results. That is needed for progress even in organisations. Keep being resilient, Ijem," he said.

His kind compliments left Ijem feeling so special, but that only attracted more animosity towards her. However, she had learnt that no matter what you do, some people will always not be satisfied. At the end of the week, they returned to school. The president was particularly happy and appreciated Ijem for the very active role she played in organising the trip. "If I have the opportunity of becoming the president again, I will gladly like to work with you," he said in appreciation of Ijem's contribution. "Imagine that most organisations that turned me down when I called for a follow-up, turned around and approved our visit when you spoke with them. What happened? Did you use a charm?" he asked, smiling at her as they stood in front of the department where the buses had discharged them. "You are an asset to anybody that has your company. Each time I went against what you advised, I had cause to reverse it and tender an apology to the house. I did that in a bid to avoid doing what you advised. You are wise, too wise for your age. I am happy we made this trip happen. Thank you once again, Ijem," he said as they had a handshake.

"It's my pleasure, Mr President. I enjoyed your vote of thanks, particularly how articulate you were and your arsenal of words. You were great out there. I am proud to work with you, Mr President," Ijem said. Both of them smiled at each other for an accomplished task and parted, each heading out to their hostels.

The proceeds from the excursion that came to the department and the university was overwhelming. There were donations of books, shelves, and other academic materials to the school from some of the organisations they visited. At the end of the tenure, accounts were presented and an audit committee set up to review what they had submitted. The books were cross-checked and Ijem was not found wanting in anyway contrary to the rumours that she had misappropriated the association's funds for personal aggrandisement.

The HOD was very happy with her. She was endeared to the HOD, the staff adviser and the priest for her smartness, uprightness and transparency in handling the association's funds.

❧ Twenty-four ❧

She continued her business as she did her final year in the university. The day she wrote her final examinations, she went gaga, she went crazy, she danced and raved in front of her webcam, making a video out of her celebration at finishing school. She could not contain herself. "At last, I am a graduate. I am a graduate of a prestigious university. I am a legend! I am ready to conquer the world. I am ready for the favour market and not the labour market. I am blessed. Thank you, Lord. Thank you, Jesus, thank you, Fr. Mmaduka for starting this journey. Thank you, Mama, thank you all that helped me come this far. Thank you, Lord!" she screamed as she danced in her room. She danced and popped a bottle of wine she received as a gift few months back. They danced and danced till their energy got sapped. She slept dreaming of a beautiful life ahead of her ...

Her joy and celebration was cut short during her final school clearance. Every graduate was expected to present all the receipts of payments of all the necessary fees paid from the first year to the final year so as to get the fees clearance certificate. Each student was also expected to present his/her library certificate showing that he/she was not owing the university any book. Other important clearance certificates come from the security department and admission department. The admission department was supposed to confirm all credentials that were presented during admission and also file in all the results obtained in the course of study. When it got to that point, Ijem Obidi's file was missing. The file was not where her classmates' files were.

She spent weeks at the admission office ransacking stacks of dusty files, looking for hers. *God, what is happening to me at this stage? I thought I could sing the song, 'The Storm is Over'? How can I get my result if my file is not found?* she cried out of frustration. She wrote letters to the appropriate authorities when she could not find it. "I think you should go home and rest. We will see to it that the file is found. It may have gotten mixed up in the course of transferring files from our former office. You know this is a new office. I am sure that was when it could have happened. I am really sorry about that. Your file would be found if you do not have any other problem of say 'forged results', the file attendant assured Ijem.

"But if this file is not found on time, my result won't be computed early and that means I might not go for my National Youth Service with the first batch," Ijem said to the assistant, worried.

"Well, I understand your feeling, but once your file is found and you pass all your courses, it would be computed and also approved by the Senate the same time with others," Mr Oguntade, the attendant, affirmed.

"But, how will I even know when it is found? We are not allowed to see our results till the evening of the award night after Senate approval. What if I get there only to realise that my name is not on the list? What happens, Sir?" Ijem asked, terrified at the possibility.

"Like I said, we will do our best provided you do not have any other problem."

Few days later, students were asked to vacate the hostels. Ijem had no option than to travel home, but unhappy. She managed to keep it from her family. She kept visiting the school to check if her file had been found, but the security did not allow the students into the administrative building to avoid mix-ups.

On the eve of the Senate sitting, students were seen flocking around the campus in fear. Nobody knew what the outcome would be. No student had seen any of their final year results. There was an air of uncertainty as the potential graduates lurked around the Senate premises. Soon the results were approved and were published later in the day. Lo and behold, Ijem's registration number was missing from the list. Ijem broke down right there. She cried hopelessly. "Why is my own always different? I am now a graduate with no result. God, please. You need to rectify this for me please!" she cried.

She went to the Head of Department's office but he was absent. She was asked to return in two days' time. She did and reported her ordeal to the Head of Department. "But every bonafide student of this institution has four files—one kept in the Department, Registry, Admission and Exams and Records, so even if your file misses at the exams and records, it is supposed to be at these other places," the HOD said. He was quite disturbed. "So, Ijem, your result was not in the list of the results published on Friday?"

"Yes, Sir!" she responded in tears.

"Don't worry, don't cry, it is not an issue so far your file is in this department." He pressed his table's bell summoning his secretary. The secretary opened the door in response. "Amadi, call the person in charge of the departmental results."

"Yes, Sir!" Amadi said, bounding off. Soon the door opened and Mr Ogu came in.

"You sent for me, Sir."

"Yes, did you compute Ijem Obidi's result?"

"No, Sir!"

"Why?"

"Sir, her results are intact but I could not retrieve her file from the Exams and Records ... I just keyed in the grades into the system but could not include it since there was no file and we were rushing to meet up with the Senate deadline ..." Mr Ogu explained.

"Her results are intact but no file? This is strange, even at Exams and Records?"

"Yes, Sir," she had no file there or rather, we could not find her file. Sir, I suggest we contact the registrar's office and admissions to see if her files are there, then we can take it from there. The Senate will sit again in three weeks and that will coincide with the day fixed for this year's award night."

"Okay, Ogu, thank you." The HOD, Prof. Akande, sat down on his chair, thought for a few seconds and said, "My dear, it is quite sad that this kind of thing can happen. But I will see to it that it is rectified. You are too good a student to be facing this kind of challenge. Don't worry although I know that you are worried. I will do my best and I assure you, it will be sorted out in no time. Your result must be published after the next senate sitting," the HOD assured Ijem.

"Thank you very much, Sir. God bless you," Ijem said.

"This kind of thing should not be happening in a university. Take my number, go home and just call me at intervals to check the progress. Don't bother coming here all the way from home."

"I already have your number, Sir. I tried calling you then but your number wasn't reachable so I thought you had changed the line."

"Oh no, I travelled to Geneva for a conference and popped into London to see my son and his family. I spent about a month outside. I returned only yesterday."

"Okay, Sir, I will be calling you. Thanks a lot."

"You are welcome, my dear," the HOD said, smiling to brighten her up.

Three weeks later, after the Senate sitting, another batch of results were published. Ijem's result was among those published. "Congratulations, Ijem, you did very well. I'll leave it as a surprise for you until you come ... see you at the award night." Prof. Akande hung up the phone.

✡ ✡ ✡ ✡ ✡

She was expectant. Prof. Akande had told her that she did well. All the students were seated with their guests, as was the tradition for the award night. Ijem trusted her HOD who had kept the result secret from her. She arrived the school in the company of her Uncle, Patty, her mother, Nneka, and her immediate younger step-sister. It was a beautiful evening, the atmosphere was right for the event. The university premises was beautified and the banquet hall was well decorated. The Vice-Chancellor and other principal officers of the university were seated with guests from other higher institutions, multinational firms, international agencies and organisations, and even governmental agencies. They were ready to present their awards to deserving students. The university music department set the stage right for the event by their wonderful renditions. After, that, all cheered and clapped in high spirits. The university orator then took the stage. "Ladies and gentlemen, we all know why we are here ... this is the kind of evening I wish never ends," she said in her opening statements. "This evening, in the presence of the movers and shakers of this country and institution, before all the graduating students, the current students and our amiable Vice-Chancellor, it is my exceptional joy to present to you, ladies and gentlemen, the most beautiful girl, the most industrious girl, the most intelligent girl, the icon of her time, a girl who has proved to be worthy in character and learning. I present to you the best graduating student of this great citadel of learning, the person holding the academic crown of this session. She is no other person than Miss Ijeabalum Maryjane Obidi!" The crowd cheered. Ijem could not believe her ears. She knew that her CGPA had been high for the four years she had been in the university. Best graduating student in her class was in order but she never reckoned that she could be the best in the university. Tears were streaming down her cheeks ... Her uncle whom she called 'Daddy' hugged her, her mother was all smiles ... She gathered herself, still shaken by the news and struggled to weave her way from where she was seated to go up to the podium. She was delirious as the Vice-Chancellor shook her hands in a warm and gripping handshake and, afterwards, handing her awards, certificates and prizes from twenty-five multinational agencies, banks, private and corporate bodies. She also took prizes for the best graduating student in her department and faculty. In all, she had fifty-nine prizes and awards. She could not contain herself. She thought, smiling furtively, *what a beautiful evening!*

The next day was the convocation. The campus was agog, overtaken by the festive mood. The premises was littered with cars, SUVs and all manner of vehicular contraptions largely brought in by visitors, friends, family relatives, guests, alumni members of the university who came for the convocation ceremony. Nnedimma was brought to attend the event. It was yet another grand outing for Ijem. She looked happy and bright wearing the academic regalia–the gown, cap and a scroll in hand.

The auditorium which was filled to its brim was soon called to order with the announcement of the arrival of the principal officers of the university, the members of the Senate, governing council, and special guests including the Vice-Chancellor and Pro-Chancellor.

The national anthem was rendered by the university's musical group, followed by the university anthem. A priest said the opening prayer and the event was declared open by the Vice-Chancellor of the university. The event commenced again with the university orator leading and mastering the ceremony.

"Congratulations to all the graduating students of our great university ... Today, we are proud of each and every one of you for your efforts throughout your stay in this institution. We believe you are leaving this great citadel of learning better than you came. In line with the motto of this institution, we want to believe that you all got the best and will be the best wherever you find yourselves. We are proudly sending you today into the world to go and make a difference. In the course of your stay here, you must have learnt some things that will help you in life, you all can differentiate between the good and the bad. You all know that you have what it takes to make great impact in your community and the wider society. We would be glad and proud to read good stories about you all and we look forward to that ...

"Now, may I have the honour of introducing to all of us here, the one person who stood out, as Yorubas would say; *Oyato!* Out of the over twelve thousand five hundred and ninety-two graduating students this academic session ... This is a very special graduating student. One who has set a record. One who has made history, and a record that will ever be in the special records of this institution. I have the pleasure to introduce this special girl, one, before whom doors will open in the future ... She is no other person than ..." the university orator stopped in her tracks, holding the audience to suspense! A moment elapsed and the audience erupted in a thunderous applause, cheering and clapping as they rose to a standing ovation even without the name of the person being mentioned. Necks were craning and turning in all directions to catch a glimpse of the girl who had made such an impact.

Those who did not know her were still stretching their necks trying to catch a glimpse of this wonderful girl who had made the university proud by establishing a new record of excellence. Just then, the university orator finally let the cat out of the bag as she raised her pitch when the ovation had died down considerably and said, "Ladies and gentlemen, join me in welcoming to the stage for her valedictory speech, a distinguished student, who will soon be turning into a legend, the most deserving of today's encomiums because of her brilliance. The overall best graduating student of this great institution, Miss Ijeabalum Maryjane Obidi!" The audience went into another round of frenzied ululation as they rose once again to their feet, clapping and cheering as the gorgeously dressed girl emerged from the right corner of the hall beaming and holding aloft her scroll and walking steadily in a measured stride to the dais. Wearing a black dress with silvery design, she was just prim and proper. Well fitted on her slim figure, the academic gown hung distinctly sweeping and swaying as she made her stride to the podium.

She smiled and waved at the cheering audience and took the last step up onto the stage as the Vice-Chancellor welcomed her with a warm handshake. She received a mixture of handshakes and warm embraces from the principal officers of the university, the deans and special guests. Thereafter, she mounted the podium and faced the audience with a beautiful and overwhelming smile.

The crowd cheered louder. She was being admired by all the guests seated on the podium. *What a combination of beauty and brain! I wish she was my daughter. Her parents must be very proud of her,* Dr Ene thought, as he hugged her. "You deserve a hug and not a handshake. I didn't know you were a student of this university," he said to her.

"Thank you very much," she mumbled.

"Dr Ene, do you remember me?" he asked her.

"Yes! Quite a surprise to see you here, Sir!" Later he would tell her that he was now the Group Managing Director of a multinational oil company called Zonelli Corp. His company had donated prizes and awards for the Best Graduating Student and he was particularly invited by the university, to grace the occasion.

"I am so overwhelmed with love and laughter that I just know that this is the happiest day of my life. To my mother and my grandmother, the two very special women in my life, I dedicate this day. I am happy you know now that your daughter is now all grown up. Both women have been my father as well as mother. Special thanks to the Almighty God for the blessings of this day." She smiled at her two mothers and thanked everybody who had helped her achieve this seemingly impossible goal of her life. Cheering resumed as she walked to her seat.

When the celebration was declared closed, many guests and friends jostled for a photograph with her. Dr Ene made it a point to feature in her pictures. He also had a word with her. "I am so proud of you, Ijem. I didn't remember you were a student of this university."

"Yes, Sir, it was after the IT that I decided to change institutions," Ijem told him.

"I am so proud of you. What about your parents?" he asked.

"My mother and grandmother are over there," she pointed.

"Okay, if you don't mind, I would love to meet them and personally congratulate them for a job well done. They are blessed to have a genius as a daughter," he said.

Bashfully, Ijem said, "Oh! Thank you so very much, Sir." He took her phone number, and gave her his complimentary card and told her to keep in touch.

"I will," she said, as he left.

The news of her graduation was all over her village. The convocation ceremony was broadcast live on the national television network. Many people from different parts of the country viewed the broadcast and so did Jack.

"How did this happen? She was not supposed to have graduated. At least not until I was satisfied. Oh, this idiot took my money, yet he did not do the job," Jack fumed as he swore under his breath. He picked up his phone and dialled a number.

"Hello!" came a voice from the other end.

"Come, Iwu, what happened? So you took my money without

doing the job? You will pay dearly for this mess!"

"Ah! Oga Jack, I am already paying dearly for doing your job. The university has relieved me of my duties. I have been sacked. The Head of her department took it upon himself to get to the root of the matter. I was able to retrieve two of her files but the third was not accessible to me. They worked with the file from the Admissions Office. I regret doing that job for you. Now see where it has landed me. I am now jobless. How much did you pay me after all and you are there threatening me?" Iwu retorted.

"Oh, that's bad news for you. But then take it easy, man. I will sort it out for you," Jack said and hung up the phone.

Twenty-five

Four months down the line, she got her NYSC deployment letter. She was ironically deployed to Zonelli Corp, the multinational corporation that Dr Ene was heading. Ijem thought, *this man again*. Continuing, she muttered, "Why must our paths cross? I know he's going to continue from where he stopped. Who knows if he would let me finish my NYSC in peace or ask for my redeployment or demand an outright rejection?"

Contrary to her worry, Dr Ene avoided her. It turned out pleasant working in such a comfortable and beautiful environment as the organisation provided.

In the course of her work, she was selected as the only Corps member among other staff that represented Zonelli Corp at an oil and gas summit in Geneva.

It was exciting for Ijem undertaking that trip. The five representatives of the corporation were conveyed to the airport with the official vehicle. They were just at the entrance of the lobby for check in when she saw somebody... *This is too good to be true. Ade!* She quickly ran over and touched him as he was briskly walking as if he was almost late for a flight. "I can't believe this," he screamed. "Look at you, you are more beautiful than ever!" They hugged. "I have called your number a million times. In fact, I memorised the number as I kept dialing it, hoping it will go through someday," he said in a light American accent. He looked polished, smarter and handsome.

"Oh, I am very sorry. I lost my phone few days after the last time we met. Thank God we met again," she said.

"Yeah, you can say that again."

"Hmm, now you have a foreign accent," she teased him.

"Yeah, don't mind me, girl. Honestly, I am so glad we met again. I thought I had lost you. I missed you so much, Ijem, I did," he said, beaming.

"I missed you too."

He moved closer to her, "Please, tell me you are still free for me."

"How do you mean, free for you?" she asked.

"Now, you are being cunning. I know you know exactly what I mean. Okay, let me shoot straight. I hope you are not married yet?"

She managed to flash him a smile as she said, "Probably not. What about you?"

"I am al-most ..." She honestly feared to hear ... married! He observed her countenance and completed his sentence, "... losing hope. But I am still very much single and seriously searching but I think my search will soon be over," he winked.

She pretended not to have read meanings into those words. "So when is your wedding date?"

"I will tell you later. But now, I have a flight to catch. I am heading to the UK but I will be back in one week. But then where are you heading to?"

"Geneva; for a summit," she said as a matter-of-fact.

"Hmm, that's nice! You now represent corporations and mingle with multinationals? Girl, you rock, congratulations!" he said, smiling.

"Thanks. It's God."

"Alright, my darling. Give me your number. The one that rings and is picked. I promise you will be my first call when I return." He teased her, adding, "When are you due back?"

"In two weeks. The conference will last for one week, but we have one week set aside for fun." They laughed as he gesticulated saying he was going to miss her. They exchanged numbers, hugged and parted.

* * * * *

On arrival from Geneva, Ade was waiting at the airport to pick her up. He dropped her off at her apartment at the staff quarters of Zonelli Corp. "I will let you rest today, Sweetheart, but we will have a lot of catching up to do ..."

"That will be so fine. You have a lot to tell me about the United States, Johns Hopkins University and so on," she said as she alighted from the car. He helped her drop her luggage inside the house, gave her a hug and left.

* * * * *

They spent time almost every evening catching up. She told him all about her life except the part that she was still somehow married to Jack.

He sponsored a birthday party for her as she told him, "I have never had a birthday bash before."

It was on a Saturday evening. She invited friends from her office, her fellow Corps members and a few of Ade's friends. After the toast, Ade did the unexpected. He popped the ultimate question which every woman wants to be asked. "Please, say yes! Will you be my wife, Ijem?" There was pin-drop silence. Suspense ...

Friends watched in anticipation. Ijem was not only shocked, she was speechless. The atmosphere, the people, the ambience and setting and the manner in which he planned it. She held back a tear, conquered her doubts and demons, to say, "Yes, yes, I will marry you, Ikem!"

He retrieved something from his pocket, asked her to give him her hands. He fitted a beautiful gold engagement ring on her finger, kissed her perfunctorily and then hugged her. The audience cheered. The DJ turned on the music louder and they danced and wined till late in the night.

Their relationship grew stronger and they started wedding

plans ... But there was still a snag. Ijem was worried that she had not quite disengaged from the betrothal and again had not told Ade of its existence. She lapsed into reverie ... *I had told my people that I didn't want to marry Jack. From the look of things, we cannot even live together. We are not compatible. He is uneducated. He reasons differently. He feels so insecure and cooks up allegations, and always puts me on the spot. I want a man I will look into his eyes and say I love you. A man that will appreciate me, and I will equally appreciate too. A man that understands me; my dreams and aspirations. A man that I will complement and we will be compatible with each other. An enlightened man. Ade is the man. I love him, and being around him makes me feel I have the world at my feet.* She smiled at the memories which Ade brought each time she thought about him. Her smile was short-lived as she broke out of her reverie to ask herself, "How do I tell Ade about Jack? I am scared of losing him. This is another serious hurdle to be crossed," she agonised.

Jack was pacing about in his room in Lagos ... "So, this girl thinks she can disgrace me. She rejected me. A whole me, Jack Nwokeike. I will teach her a lesson. A lesson her generation will never forget. I will show her pepper. Let her wed let's see." He swore to disrupt the upcoming wedding he had gotten wind of which Ijem was planning.

On the wedding day, the bride arrived the church, friends and well wishers were all present. The priest was even in the vestry, waiting. They waited a little longer than usual yet the groom had not turned up. Someone came to whisper to Ijem that she sighted Jack in the church premises.

One hour past the scheduled time, a message reached the

priest about the groom's absence. The priest briskly strode into the church to announce to the surprise of everyone that the wedding had been put on hold till further notice. "The groom has suddenly been hospitalised as I speak. It is unfortunate. We are sorry for the inconvenience but God knows the best." Ijem fell on the pew, she was promptly rushed to the hospital. Two hours later, she was revived. The news of the cancelled wedding went viral. The wedding audience dispersed except very close friends and family members of Ade and Ijem who all rushed to the hospital.

They all panicked as the doctors could not tell them what exactly was wrong with Ade. They were also denied access to see him. It was feared he could be dead. Ijem cried her eyes out.

Jack and his group returned home disappointed. "Well, at least the wedding couldn't hold. If the sickness didn't stop him, I could have. I even like the fact that the silly girl fainted in the presence of everyone on the so-called wedding day," Jack said mockingly.

Nneka entered the ward where Ijem was sitting on the bed. "Ijem, I am really sorry that this is happening on this day of all days. It is very bad indeed. But I want to tell you something but on the condition ..."

Startled, Ijem asked, "What condition?"

"I say on the condition that you dress up now and clean up your face, make up and look good, then I will tell you the rest of what I had wanted to tell you. Ijem was disappointed and started sobbing again.

"Mother, what is the essence of dressing up? I don't have another cloth here to wear. Can somebody get home and get me another dress because I don't want to be seen wearing this wedding gown out of this hospital. Please, Mother!"

"Don't worry, just wear the one that is available now. I will send somebody to fetch another dress. Please, dress up. The priest is outside. He wants to see you and he won't see you naked. Moreover, he cannot wait till somebody goes home and returns with a change of clothes for you, please," Nneka begged.

"Okay, Mama," she reluctantly wore her wedding dress. Her chief bride's maid cleaned up her face and applied some make-up.

She looked as radiant as she was in the morning except that her eyes were puffy and pale. Nneka led the way, and she followed with her maid holding her train. She was led to the hall of the hospital. To her surprise, there were many people seated there, smiling up to her. She became confused the more. The Rev. Father wants to celebrate mass to pray with us and also for Ade's quick recovery," Nneka whispered to her as she led her to her seat.

"Close your eyes, let us pray," the priest urged. Eyes closed in anticipation for the prayers to be said ... Just then, Ijem felt a figure beside her but knew her chief bride's maid was beside her just that it felt like a bigger figure ... and then there was a whisper in her ears of someone saying, "I love you, my angel." She opened her eyes to behold Ade; all dressed up for the wedding. He was not looking ill, had no injury, and appeared fresh. She was speechless. She opened her mouth to ask a question or say something, but could not say a thing.

"I'm so sorry not to have let you into this plan. It was a plot, baby. I learnt about Jack although you didn't tell me. I learnt about him and his sinister plans just as I was about to come to the church for the wedding. The priest was told. And the only way to avert trouble was to let it happen the way it did. I am so sorry. I did what I thought was best for us. He planned to disrupt our wedding in the morning," he explained as he hugged her very tight for a while.

Eventually in a solemn ceremony, the priest joined them in marriage. Her pale and puffy eyes regained their sparkle. The wedding held that same day but in the evening as against the morning period when it was slated.

182

The reception was held right there at the hospital. As she was about to enter the car to proceed for their honeymoon, a young man approached her pointing at a new black Range Rover Evoque parked in front of the car they were about to enter and delivered a big brown envelop to her.

She opened it; there was a car key, an address of a terrace duplex with the house keys somewhere in Maitama, Abuja. A cheque which had the sum of twenty million naira written on it and a note. Ade stood behind her as she brought out the contents of the envelop, they both stared at each other astonished. She read the note. 'Congratulations, my dear! I am so proud of you. I wish you a happy married life. I am deeply sorry for everything. If only you will ever forgive me for what I did to your mother! The heartaches! I only discovered who you are when I went to congratulate your mother on your convocation day. If only you will believe, and accept me; I am yours sincerely, your father, Dr Ene.'

Igbo Glossary

Chime e	An exclamation, my God ee
Nne	Mother
Agbala	An itchy plant
Ncha nkota	Native black soap made from palm oil and ash
Mpanaka	A local kerosene lamp
Kachifo	Good night
Akpata	A long local broom for sweeping outdoor
Igbegiri	Stumps of palm frond
Okpoga	A local wooden stool
Biko	Please
Mkpa-aki	Search for palm nut
Ukpaka	Oil bean seed
Aki	Palm kernel
Nwam	My child
Ukwa	Breadfruit
Okwuma	Shea butter
Apa	Wound scars
Utazi	A bitter green vegetable
Ugba	Cooked and sliced oil bean seed ready for consumption
Iri ji	New yam festival
Mkpi	He-goat
Achicha	Sun dried plantain strips
Ugani	Famine season, the intervening period before the harvesting season.
Ngwa nu	Come on
Ite-igwe	Round cast iron cooking pot
Onugbu	Bitter leaf
Bologi	West African perennial climbing plant that is used as a potherb
Inyomoha	Married women association
I nu go	Have you heard?

Akpu	Cassava foo foo
Ofe onugbu	Bitter leaf soup
Nno nu	You are welcome
Akara	Bean cake
Egbuo m	Killed me
Ndo	Sorry
Mama nnukwu	Grandmother
Ji anunu	Local yam
Anyu	Bologi fruit
Ugboguru	Bologi leaves
Mbughu	Grated and boiled cocoyam delicacy
Iti	Dullard
Umunna	Kinsmen
Obubuo	Vegetable maggots
Santa Nwegbe	Holy saint

Proverb

O bialu be onye abiagbuna ya,

   May one's visitor not constitute a problem,

O nabakwa mkpumkpu apuna ya.

   so that on his departure he will not leave with a hunchback.[1]

---

[1] Chinua Achebe: https://www.igboguide.org/guests /igbo-proverbs.htm

French Glossary

L'argon, c'est finis	Money is finished
Je suis ton frère maintenant	I am your brother now
Je n'ai pas parles bien l'anglais	I don't speak English very well
si'l te plait	Please
Mon pere	My Father
L'argon du Nigerian	Nigerian currency
Mon pere a' habites a la Suisse	My father lives in Switzerland

Kraftgriots

Also in the series (FICTION) (*continued*)

Ibrahim Buhari: *A Quiet Revolutionary* (2012)

Onyekachi Peter Onuoha: *Idara* (2012)

Akeem Adebiyi: *The Negative Courage* (2012)

Onyekachi Peter Onuoha: *Moonlight Lady* (2012)

Temitope Obasa: *Strokes of Life* (2012)

Chigbo Nnoli: *Save the Dream* (2012)

Florence Attamah-Abenemi: *A Bouquet of Regrets* (2013)

Ikechukwu Emmanuel Asika: *Tamara* (2013)

Aire Oboh: *Branded Fugitives* (2013)

Emmanuel Esemedafe: *The Schooldays of Edore* (2013)

Abubakar Gimba: *Footprints* (2013)

Emmanuel C.S. Ojukwu: *Sunset for Mr Dobromir* (2013)

Million John: *Amongst the Survivors* (2013)

Onyekachi Peter Onuoha: *My Father Lied* (2013)

Razinat T. Mohammed: *Habiba* (2013)

Onyekachi Peter Onuoha: *The Scream of Ola* (2013)

Oluwakemi Omowaire: *Dead Roses* (2013)

Chidubem Iweka: *So Bright a Darkness* (2014)

Asabe K. Usman: *Destinies of Life* (2014)

Stan-Collins Ubaka: *A Cry of Innocence* (2014)

Data Osa Don-Pedro: *Behind the Mask* (2014)

Stanley Ekwugha: *Your Heart My Home* (2014)

Yemi Ajagbe: *The Triumph of Childhood Trials* (2014)

Ndubuisi George: *Woes of Ikenga* (2014)

Nwanneka Obioma Nwala: *Wives on the Cross* (2014)

Ebere Ezike: *The Housemaid* (2014)

Emmanuel C. S. Ojukwu: *A Whiff of Kahara* (2014)

Bizuum Yadok: *King of the Jungle* (2014)

Onyekachi Peter Onuoha: *The Fears of Mama* (2014)

Ikenna Nwadike: *The Holy Heist* (2014)

Chukwu Adindu: *Destined Not to Arrive* (2015)

rome aboh: *above the rubble* (2015)

Terhemba Shija: *The Siege, the Saga* (2015)

Emmanuel Iwuno: *The Broken Path* (2015)

Mazi Sam Ohuabunwa: *The Port Harcourt Volunteer* (2015)

Onyekachi Peter Onucha: *Identity* (2015)

Gloria Ernest-Samuel: *Iheoma My Dear* (2016)

Clement Chukwuka Idegwu: *Right to be Angry* (2016)

Ibe Ifeanyi: *The Urashi Conquest* (2016)

Phil Ngozi Nwoko: *Dancing with the Ostrich* (2016)

Aoiri Obaigbo: *The Wretched Billionaire* (2016)

Kaase Fyanka: *The Golden Sword of Dragon* (2016)

Data Osa Don-Pedro: *I am Somebody* (2016)

Jerry Alagbaoso: *Officers and Men* (2016)

Liwhu Betiang: *The Rape of Hope* (2016)
Lola Akande: *What it Takes* (2016)
Zainab Aikali: *Invisible Borders* (2016)
Tony Nwaka: *Mountain of Yesterday* (2017)
Law Ikay Ezeh: *Your Church My Shrine* (2017)
Oselumhense Anetor: *Triumph of Innocence* (2017)
Abubakar Gimba: *Sacred Apples* (2017)
Orlando Dokubo: *The Arm-Twist* (2017)